Some Strange ~~...~~

Kitty The Hare

The Famous Travelling Woman of Ireland

VICTOR O'D. POWER

THE MERCIER PRESS
DUBLIN and CORK

The Mercier Press Limited
4 Bridge Street, Cork
25 Lower Abbey Street, Dublin 1

ISBN 0 85342 661 9

Printed by Litho Press Co., Midleton, Co. Cork.

Contents

Biddy the Matchmaker

Wisha, faith, 'tis time for us to have a good laugh tonight, imbeersa! So I'm going to tell ye all about Nannie Ryan's matchmaking, and 'tis worth your while to listen to old Kitty; for 'tis a droll story enough, so it is.

'Twas given up, why, to Nannie Ryan to be the purtiest young girl going into Kilcash chapel of a Sunday. I think I never, in all my rambles, saw such a pair of coaxing blue eyes in anyone's head as Nannie's were, the craythur, and she had elegant silky brown hair, with a wave in it, and sometimes, when the sun was shining on it, you'd swear it was red and sometimes yella, and it all curling around her forehead in little rings.

And, sure, as purty as Nannie Ryan was, she was just as nice and as good in every other way; so 'twas no wonder at all that everyone was fond of her around her south Tipperary home, and Dick Ryan, her father, was cract alive about her, because she was the dead image of her mother, poor Mary Maher, who died, God help us, a few weeks after Nannie was born. Ye can guess for yourselves how fond of little Nannie Dick Ryan was when he never put a stepmother over her, and he a fine, hearty young man at the time poor Mary died, and many a girl in the parish only too eager, why, to snap him up if he'd take her; for he had as rich a farm as you'd find in all the Golden Vale—as they call that part of the country down there. So Dick Ryan's sister, Anne, looked after young Nannie, and the child grew up, as I tell you, to be a credit to the family, and the neighbours were all saying among themselves that surely to goodness Nannie Ryan would be making a great match of it some day or other, and they were all wondering who the young man would be at all, at all.

And the first time myself rambled around the Kilcash

side and strolled into Dick Ryan's farmhouse Nannie was eighteen years old, and the very minute I laid eyes on her my heart went out to her, somehow, and nothing could equal all the kindness and good-nature she showed me that night. Didn't she make down a bed for me in her own little room in the loft, and before I knew where I was in the morning wasn't she alongside of my bed with a cup of tea and a slice of bread and butter in her hands. And, 'Drink this now, Kitty, woman,' says she, 'and eat this morsel of bread, and then,' says she, 'you can take another sleep. Sure you'll be long enough up and you must be dead tired from the roads, God help you!' says the warm-hearted, friendly little girl.

And from that out, herself and myself were as thick as could be, awonomsa, and she'd open out her heart to me whenever I'd stroll the way, and 'tis many's the shining white shilling she'd slip into my pocket, out of the egg-money, and didn't she put a span new dress on me, one Christmas time, and an elegant new cap trimmed with satin ribbon. Well, why, but here's my story for you. Sure, if I kept praising Nannie Ryan, I wouldn't feel the time passing till morning.

I'm just after telling ye what the neighbours used to be saying to one another about Nannie's grand match; and 'tis many a young farmer in the parish they were naming as a suitable 'Clian isthock' for Dick Ryan; for you see, as Dick had no son to step into his shoes, he was looking out for a son-in-law to live in the house and afterwards to own the farm.

And, the Lord save us, who did he pitch on, do you think, but one Mr Timothy Kearney, a returned Yank, who was after spending up to thirty years in America; so ye many guess he wasn't the sort of a man that poor Nannie Ryan, or any other young girl, would fancy for a husband. And just after Dick Ryan first drew down this match to Nannie, myself chanced to ramble to the farmhouse, one August evening, and in the old boreen leading to the farmyard didn't I meet Nannie herself, and she walking along, all alone, and her eyes red with the dint of crying. And, faith, when she spied me coming she ran to meet me and she threw her arms round my neck and she up and she told me all her troubles from beginning to end, the poor little girl.

And, 'Oh, Kitty,' says she, 'I'd sooner beg the world with a boy I'd love than be tied to a man like Mr Kearney. Sure, he's sixty, if he's an hour,' says she, 'and the big, pompous red face of him, and his grey bristles sticking out of his bullet head, for all the world like a granioge's,' says she.

'But because he has plenty of cash, my father and my aunt are after fixing on him as a match for me,' says she; 'but faith, if they are, Kitty,' says she, 'I'll be too clever for them, so I will! And already I'm after making up a plan of my own to get out of this business altogether—and I expect to know this very evening,' says she, 'whether 'twill be a success or whether it won't.'

And when I asked her some questions didn't she tell me then that she was after putting her case in the hands of Biddy Cadogan herself, the south Tipperary matchmaker, who was well-known at that time from one end of the country to the other.

'And I told Biddy to find out a suitable match for me,' says Nannie, 'and I gave her my photograph that I got taken in Tramore last June, and I'm expecting her back this very evening with some news for me, so I am,' says Nannie, 'for 'tis over a week ago since she started on her journey.'

And just while Nannie and myself were chatting like this in the boreen, up comes a fine, handsome, black-eyed young man, with a pleasant smile on his face, and he holding a bow of blue ribbon in his hand. And, 'Begging your pardon, Nannie,' says he, 'but I'm after finding this bow of ribbon this evening stuck in the furze-bushes just above the five-acre field,' says he, and a deludhering twinkle in his black eyes, 'I said I'd bring it to you, safe and sound, girl.'

'And faith, sure, it is mine right enough, Wattie,' says Nannie, and she blushing like a red rose, 'Aunt Anne sent me to search the furze-brake for eggs today,' says she. 'Some of the hens are laying out,'says she, 'and I missed the bow when I came back. Thank you, Wattie, boy,' says she. 'I'm glad you found it.'

And when the black-eyed young man passed up the boreen I asked Nannie who he was, and she told me he was one Wattie Brien, a native of north Tipperary away by the Devil's Bit, and that her father, Dick Ryan, was after hiring Wattie just a few days before as a servant-boy.

'And he's the smartest, best-boy we ever had here,' says Nannie. 'My father is cract about him already, and so is Aunt Anne.'

'Wisha, that's all very fine, Nannie, alay,' says myself to her; 'but keep it before your mind, my girl,' says I, 'that Wattie is only your father's servant-boy, and don't let him be making too free with you,' says I. 'For, if you do, maybe you'd be sorry for it when a suitable match turns up for you, one of these days.'

And, faith, the words were barely out of my mouth when a footstep came down the boreen right behind us, and when we looked round, lo, and behold ye! there was Biddy Cadogan herself. At this time I'm telling ye about, Biddy Cadogan was a wiry, keen-eyed little old woman, well-dressed and as neat as a new pin. She always wore a hooded cloak and a frilled white cap, just like mine, with a bright red-and-black shawl around it. And, faith, no wonder she'd be well-dressed, imbeersa; for, by all accounts, her trade of matchmaking brought her in lashings of money every year.

So she called Nannie a-one side; and, faith, if she did, she had a piece of good news for her, too! Wasn't she after making out a grand young man for Nannie—one Maurice Gleeson, the second son of Paul Gleeson of the Orchard Farm, away by Knockroe, about a dozen miles from Kilcash. And Maurice Gleeson was after falling in love with Nannie's photograph, Biddy told her, and as soon as ever he could leave home he was going to come on her to Kilcash. But his brother, Willie, was after getting a fall from one of the horses and he had to lie up for a bit; so Maurice Gleeson couldn't very well leave home till Willie was all right again. But, with God's help, as Biddy said, that wouldn't be long. So, faith, poor Nannie then and there took a red handkerchief out of her pocket, and in the corner of it she had five half-crowns tied up.

'Well, Biddy,' says she, 'you're after doing your business well—so far, anyway,' says she, 'and, sure, 'tis only fair to pay you what I promised you, and I only wish I could afford to give you more,' says Nannie. 'But 'twas hard enough on me, so it was,' says the poor little girl, 'to save this much itself out of the egg-money. And here it is for you now,' says she, and she handing her the five half-crowns into her fist. 'And if I'm married to this Maurice Gleeson,' says she, 'I won't forget who I'm to thank for the match, Biddy, never you fear!'

And after a few more words together the pair of them parted and Biddy Cadogan took the short cut across the fields to Brittas, where she had a little cabin of her own; and faith, after this evening Nannie got into great spirits again for a bit, though Mr Kearney used to call over every day to have a chat with her, and he was right sure that Nannie would marry him and Dick Ryan and her Aunt Anne thought the same. And Nannie was in such glee over the thought of the fine young man that Biddy Cadogan was after making off for her that she didn't seem to care a pin what she said to Mr Kearney or what he thought, why, and 'twas often, when I saw the two of them together, at this time, that I said to myself Nannie was in the wrong to be so sweet with Timothy Kearney when she had no notion of marrying him in the end. Though, faith, like that, I couldn't blame her for not liking old Timothy; a big, fat, purse-proud stuck-up bundle he was, with a gold chain as thick as a rope across his body and rings on his big, red fingers and his face the colour of a boiled lobster, and he always panting and blowing for shortness of wind he was that stout.

And, sure, he thought no girl in her senses could say 'No' to himself and his money, and he'd as soon fancy that Nannie Ryan was making a fool of him as that the world was coming to an end.

Now this was all very fine for a week or two; but, begannies, five weeks went by and still there was no sign of Maurice Gleeson turning up, good nor bad, and Mr Kearney was trying to force Nannie to name the day she'd be satisfied to marry himself, and Dick Ryan and his sister Anne, nagging at the little girl morning, noon and night, and Biddy Cadogan—to crown it all—after starting off miles away into the County Kilkenny, to fix up another match for one of the 'customers'. And so, at long last, why, Nannie got desperate, the poor craythur, and she said to herself that 'twas making a fool of her Biddy Cadogan was all the time, just to get hold of her money, and that there was no such person at all as Maurice Gleeson, or, if there was, that he had no intention of coming to the Kilcash borders to make a match with herself.

And, faith, while she was in this frame of mind, what do ye think, but didn't my brave Wattie Brien come at the soft side of poor Nannie, and he told her he was dying in love with her and he begged of her to make a runaway match of it with himself!

'Sure, we'll have to take to the road, Nannie girl,' says Wattie to her, 'for we'll have no business in staying around here, if once you'll consent to be my wife. But the world is wide,' says Wattie, 'and thanks be to God, I have plenty of my savings laid by to pay for our two tickets to New York.'

And, faith, 'twas no good for Nannie to be letting on that she didn't like Wattie Brien, for she did like him, if he was only a servant-boy itself, and she always liked him, and he always liked her from the instant minute they first clapped eyes on each other's faces, why!

And just at this very time, while the poor girl was sorely upset in her mind didn't Biddy Cadogan come the way again, and one day in September, when Nannie was all alone in the farmhouse and Dick Ryan and Wattie Brien gone to Carrick with the horse-and-car, and Anne Ryan after crossing the field with old Judy Maher, the hen-woman, didn't my brave Biddy ramble into the kitchen where Nannie, looking down in the mouth enough, the poor craythur, was darning a stocking, and she singing a sad little lilt of a song all to herself. And, faith, when she caught sight of Biddy she tossed the stocking out of her hand and she turned on the matchmaker, and if she didn't give her a fine hearing leave me alone, why!

'Isn't it a nice way you're managing this business for me, Biddy Cadogan,' says Nannie, and she in a right fury, and no wonder she would, too. 'Faith, if that's the sort of matchmaker you are,' says she, ''tis surprising to me, so it is, that anyone is fool enough to have any dealings with you at all, at all! And after I opening my heart to you,' says Nannie, 'and begging of you to find a suitable boy for me in your rambles, and you come and tell me all about Maurice Gleeson of Knockroe, and so forth, there's a whole five weeks,' says she, 'after going by and not a single word ever since from Maurice Gleeson!'

And, 'Aisy now, child of grace!—aisy now, wouldn't you!' says Biddy Cadogan and she puffing away at her dhudeen.

'Yerra, to the divil with your "Aisy now," Biddy Cadogan!' cries Nannie, and she lepping up like a mad thing. 'Do you think I'm a proper oanshough, or what?' says she. 'While you're "Aisy now-ing" here am I,' says she, 'fighting and scolding and screeching and bawling all day long, with the dint of the persecution and crucifying I'm getting from my father and Aunt Anne.

'And this very day,' says she, 'didn't my old saucepan of a Timothy Kearney come in here and force a promise out of my father that I'd be his wife next month for a certain fact and he's to come over again this evening to fix up the business, he said. And to make matters worse,' says she, 'I'd swear fifty oaths 'tain't love for me bringing him here at all,' says she, 'so it ain't; but he thinks the old place a comfortable corner to spend the last few years of his life in and to have me nurse himself and his stiff old bones,' says she, 'to the end of the chapter!

'I'd like my job, wouldn't I, Biddy Cadogan!' says she, 'yourself and your "Aisy now!" But faith, I'll take the law into my own hands from this day forward,' says she, 'and I'm planning out something this minute that will surprise all of ye, when ye'll find it out! Wait awhile!' says she, 'and the divil's cure to ye, that's all I say!'

And when those words came out of her lips, why, Biddy clapped the pipe into her pocket and lepped up off the settle with the dint of excitement.

And 'Saints and angels protect us!' says she. 'Sure, it can't be that the whisper I heard this very evening, and I crossing the hill down from Corrigaloo, is the fact truth? Oh, wirrasthrue! wirrasthrue!' says she and she clapping her hands together. 'Sure, you're not going to run away are you, Nannie,' says she, 'with your father's servant-

12

boy, Wattie Brien?'

And, 'Whether I am, or whether I'm not,' says Nannie, ''tis my own business so it is, Biddy Cadogan, and 'tis equal to you. So you can go your road now, my honest woman,' says Nannie, 'and I'll go mine, from this out!'

And, faith, before Biddy had time to make her answer in came Anne Ryan herself, Nannie's aunt—a thin, sharp-looking woman, of about fifty, with her grey hair made up in a black velvet net; and she seemed to be in a mortal hurry altogether, why, and she panting and gasping, and she coming in.

And, 'Listen here, Nannie,' says she, 'just and I crossing the kiln-field,' says she, 'I spied Mr Kearney coming up the boreen. He'll be here in a minute or two,' says she. 'So now, Nannie, be said by me once and for all. Your father and myself are bent on this match,' says she. ''Tis no good for you to be kicking up your heels, and behaving like an oanshough,' says she; and, with that, she turned to Biddy Cadogan. 'Am I right, Biddy woman, or am I wrong?' says she.

And, 'May the Lord direct the decent poor girl to do what's best for herself, Miss Anne!' says Biddy the old villain, and she ducking her head, with her two eyes fixed on the floor.

And, just and she saying it, in comes Mr Timothy Kearney, sure enough, and he dressed so grand as you like, with a buncheen of red roses stuck in his coat, and he shaping about like a young bucko on the look out for a sweetheart, why! And, faith, Anne Ryan, after a few civil words to him, went out of the kitchen and took Biddy with her, so as that the lovers, moryeh, might be left to themselves; and, if she did, why, Nannie turned on Mr Timothy Kearney, like a spitfire and if she didn't riddle him, I don't know what to say, begannies!

'How dare you come near me, you old Trick-o'-the-

Loop, you!' says Nannie, and she in a mad fury all out. 'I wouldn't marry you, Mr Kearney,' says she, 'if there wasn't another man to be got from here to the Rock of Cashel. And if you were as rich again,' says she. 'I think you have a deal of impudence, so I do,' says she, 'to come here—an old shaver, like yourself,' says she, 'that could nearly be my own grandfather,' says she, 'and to ask a young girl like me to be your wife.

'Wisha, in the name of goodness now,' says she, 'what would I marry you for at all, at all?' says she. 'Is it, let me ask you,' says she, 'for the divarshion of nursing you every day till the end of your life?' says she. 'Is it light all out you are, or what?' says she. 'Do you think I'm tired of my life so soon,' says she, 'to saddle myself with an old, grey-headed, withered divil of a man that ought to be down on his two knees praying for a happy death,' says she, 'instead of looking out, at his time of life, for a wife,' says she.

And, faith, when he heard all this out of her, Mr Kearney flew into a rage altogether—and sure, to tell nothing but the truth, no wonder he would, why!

And, 'Not another syllable out of your lips, you ill-mannered, violent-tempered stag!' says he. 'I guess I'll soon bring you to your senses, though,' says he. 'I'll go along the Carrick road right away,' says he, 'and I'll meet your father and complain to him,' says he, 'of your outrageous language and conduct, you little snake!' says he.

'Yerra, man dear, be off with you, out of my sight,' says Nannie, 'and don't stop running,' says she, ''till you meet with him, and if you happen to fall over your nose,' says she, 'don't wait to get up! Away with you now, my decent man,' says she. 'Don't you be delaying. Fair weather after you,' says she, and he running out like a lunatic out of her sight, 'and snow to your heels , you old skillet!' says she. And, faith, he wasn't long gone out, so he wasn't, when in ran Wattie Brien, and his two black eyes fairly lepping out of his head.

And, 'Nannie, Nannie girl,' says he, 'there milia murther going on outside in the stable,' says he. 'Sure didn't Mr Kearney meet us just at the gate of the baan,' says he, 'and he black in the face with the dint of rage and fury,' says he; 'and he up and told your father the way you treated him this evening,' says Wattie Brien, 'and all the insulting things you said to him; and when we reached the yard there was your Aunt Anne waiting for us,' says Wattie, 'and now the three of them are outside in the stable, all talking together, the Lord save us,' says he, 'like three magpies that would be chattering mad,' says he. 'And I just heard your father saying this minute,' says he, 'that you'll have to marry Mr Kearney early next month—that he'd end up the business at wanst,' says he, 'and put an end to all this botheration!' says Wattie.

'Faith, then, he's mistaken, if he said that,' says Nannie, 'for I'll never marry Mr Kearney,' says she. 'No —not if he was hung round with gold and jewels,' says she.

And, faith, when she said that, didn't my brave Wattie pick up his spirit at last, and didn't he ask her, plain and straight, to run away with himself that very same night to an aunt's house of his, he said, and they could go on to Queenstown from there and out to New York together to be married. And, awonomsa, if he did, Nannie wasn't the girl to spoil the sport, I'm telling ye, and she gave her consent to what he asked her, and he threw his arms around her neck and he was just in the act of kissing her—the rogue of the world!—when, the Lord save us, didn't Mr Kearney himself look in through the kitchen winda and spot what was going on within! And if he did, why, in with him to the kitchen, like a mad bull atop of them, and Dick and Anne Ryan and

Biddy Cadogan at his heels; and, sure, at that same minute, just as if it was to be, didn't myself ramble into the house, and I not knowing what was going on there at all, at all!

And, 'Isn't this nice, decent conduct, Nannie Ryan,' Mr Kearney cries, and he panting with fury, 'to be in this servant-boy's arms, you shameless creature,' says he, 'and he hugging and kissing you,' says he, 'and you hugging and kissing him!' says he.

And, faith, when he said that, didn't Nannie plant herself right before them all, with her two arms folded across her breast, and her two eyes shining like coals of fire, why!

'And who has a better right to hug and kiss me, if it comes to that,' says she, 'than the same Wattie Brien? For he's the only boy in the wide world,' says she, 'that I ever cared a thraneen about, or ever will!

'And I'm just after promising to marry him,' says she, as bold as brass. 'We settled it all just before ye came in now out of the stable. I'm going to America with Wattie at once,' says she, 'and then nayther of us will be a trouble to ye all any longer.'

And when she said this, glory be to God, Dick Ryan began to clap his hands, and his sister Anne nearly fell fainting into Mr Kearney's arms, and, 'Biddy, do you hear that?' says she, to Biddy Cadogan. 'What do you think of that, Biddy?' says she, and she hardly able to speak.

'As I said awhile ago, Miss Anne,' says Biddy, and her tongue in her cheek, why, 'may the Lord direct the decent girl for the best!'

And Anne Ryan began to clap her hands as well as Dick, and Mr Kearney with his two arms around her trying to console her as well as he could; and Dick turned on Wattie Brien and told him to quit the house that very minute or he'd break every bone in his body, and in the middle of all the pilimaloo didn't Biddy Cadogan, all of a sudden, look out through the kitchen winda, and, if she did, she let a cry out of her and shook her hand at all of them to keep them silent.

And, 'Whisht, whisht, let ye!' says Biddy. 'Here's Father John Mulcahy the parish priest of Knockroe, and he running across the yard out of the rain!'

And when Wattie Brien heard her saying this he started back and got as red as a turkey-cock, and, faith, sure enough, in came Father John Mulcahy himself—a fine, handsome, portly priest, God bless him!—and he having a riding-coat on him and top-boots, with spurs in them, and a whip in one hand, and he shaking the rain off of his hat with the other.

And, 'God save all here!' says Father John. 'I was riding home from Glenbower,' says he, 'when my mare cast a shoe, so I left her below at the forge,' says he, 'and ran up here for shelter.'

And just and he saying this, why, didn't he look around the kitchen and faith, if he did, he spotted Wattie Brien in the corner back of the dresser; and he let a cry of surprise out of him, for all the world as if he was looking at a ghost.

And, 'Glory be to God, Maurice Gleeson,' says he. 'Is it yourself that's in it,' says he, 'or am I dreaming? Where in the world,' says he, 'are you hiding yourself for the past five or six weeks?' says he.

And, with that, sure they all started and looked at one another and looked at Wattie Brien, and Anne Ryan had like to faint all out this time, only Mr Kearney catching a hold of her again.

And then, faith, Biddy Cadogan began to laugh out loud and to clap her hands, and 'The whole truth is out at last,' says she. 'And sure it couldn't come out at a better time,' says she, 'if we were after planning it all beforehand, so it couldn't. Divil a better,' says she, as well as she could speak with the laughing.

'I guess you're all gone crazy,' says Mr Kearney. 'Who may "Maurice Gleeson" be, when he's at home?' says he.

'I'll soon tell you that, Mr Kearney,' says Father John. 'Maurice Gleeson is one of the finest young men in my parish. He's the second son of Mr Paul Gleeson, of The Orchard Farm—as rich a place as you'll find in all the Golden Vale. That's who Maurice Gleeson is, when he's at home,' says Father John, 'though, faith, I'm in the dark still,' says he, 'as to who he is, or what he is when he's here!'

And with that, awonomsa, didn't 'Wattie Brien' himself come forward to Father John and he told him all about the matter from start to finish, and a droll story it was, begannies. Sure, he was the divil all out, to think of doing it at all.

'Biddy Cadogan there came to me about six weeks ago, Father John,' says he, 'to make a match between me and Nannie Ryan there. And the minute I looked at Nannie's photograph,' says he, 'I fell in love with her, Father John. So I told Biddy I'd try my chances with Nannie Ryans's people for certain and without delay too.

'And then, Father John,' says he, 'when I thought quietly over the matter, I said to myself that I'd like to find out, on the sly, first and foremost, ' says he, 'what sort the girl really was, and what sort her people were,' says he, 'before I came forward openly to ask her father for her,' says he. 'I reasoned it out in this way, Father John,' says he. 'If I went in my own name to Dick Ryan's of Kilcash, says I to myself, sure they'd all have their best side out; but I want to see every side of them, says I to myself. I want to see them on Monday as well as Sunday—in their old clothes, as well as in their new!

'So I hit on the plan, Father John,' say he,' to hire as a

servant-boy with Dick Ryan, and, faith, if I did, I carried it out, too, through a chum of mine in Carrick,' says he, 'and then I came here calling myself "Wattie Brien",' says he, 'and the divil the one of them all knew the truth of the matter only Biddy Cadogan alone. But I warned her, for her life, not to betray me. And this very evening, Father John,' says he, 'I was intending to tell them the whole truth of the story!'

And you'd think Father John would kill himself laughing when he heard this story, and "Tis an old saying, Maurice,' says he, and he clapping Maurice Gleeson (for we must give him his right name now) on the back, 'never to buy a pig in a bag; and sure, one might also say never judge a girl,' says he, 'in her Sunday clothes. If you want to know her,' says he, 'as she really and truly is, see her in her working everyday trim,' says he, 'and with her working everyday manners. And if she can stand that test,' says he, 'she can stand anything, faith!— and all is well,' says Father John.

So, begannies, the whole affair was patched up, then and there, and Dick Ryan shook hands with Maurice and forgave him for all, and Anne Ryan was still so upset over all the shocks she was after getting, the craythur, that only for Mr Kearney's arm being around her 'tis likely she couldn't stand at all, why!

And, faith, Father John—for he was a droll priest ever and always—spotted the pair of them, and, if he did, didn't he call Biddy a-one-side, and says he to her, with a wink at Mr Kearney and Anne Ryan: 'I say, Biddy,' says he, 'why not have an eye to business in that quarter?' says he. 'Why not secure a second batch of customers, as you're on the spot? A nice, suitable pair they'd be, too,' says he, 'and not too old to try on the "matrimonial halter", as old Larry Macnamara used to call it,' says he, and he striving to keep in his laughter, why!

'Faith, I'll have a try at them, anyway, your reverence,' says Biddy Cadogan. 'Sure, worse nor fail I can't,' says she. 'And by the same token,' says she, 'poor Mr Kearney was badly treated by Nannie here,' says she. 'Whisper, Father John! Didn't my prime old laddo,' says she, 'think he was going to secure the little girl himself for a wife, I thank you!' says Biddy. 'So, faith, he'd want a bit of sticking-plaster for his wounded heart, your reverence,' says Biddy and her tongue half way out, the vagabone, 'and, sure, where could he find a better bit of sticking-plaster than Miss Anne Ryan herself,' says Biddy.

And away with her to the pair of them and the Lord knows if she didn't work the point while you'd be saying 'knife' and didn't Mr Kearney bring Anne Ryan forward, and he holding her by the hand as if she was a little thackeen of fifteen or sixteen, and says he, with a leer at her out of the corner of his eye: 'Waal, I guess, good people,' says he, 'if I can't get Nannie, I'll take Annie,' says he. 'We're after settling everything,' says he, 'and we'll be married the week after next.'

And so they were, imbeersa, and Nannie and Maurice were married on the very same day.

And, faith, the two marriages turned out as lucky as ever I heard tell of anywhere; and sure, 'tis myself ought to know that if anyone could, for 'tis often I rambled to both their houses afterwards, and in all the County Tipperary you wouldn't find two more properous vanithees than Nannie Gleeson and her Aunt Anne, Timothy Kearney's wife. God bless the pair of them tonight.

The Brothers

Away in north Kerry, a few weeks ago, I was passing the lonely graveyard of Toumpleen-Breedha; and the story of the two Mahony brothers came back just as I was often hearing my mother telling all about it, in the long years gone by. About a mile and a half west of Toumpleen-Breedha the Mahony's fine old farmhouse stands in a sheltered hollow of the hills, with a belt of big trees sheltering it from the fierce storms blowing up from the sea.

And at this time I'm going to tell ye about, mossa, there was no one left in the old family home only the eldest boy, Stephen Mahony; his father and mother were dead and buried for some years and his two sisters married and settled down ten miles away, and his only brother, Frank, after running away from home the very week after their mother's death.

Both boys were cract alive about their poor mother, but they were always in dread of their father, awonomsa; because, like many another man of a house, Jeremiah Mahony was a hard, tyrannical man to his children and to his wife, and the home was unbearable to Frank the instant minute his poor mother was carried out of it and buried in the lonesome graveyard of Toumpleen-Breedha, among the wild hills to the east of the Mahony's home. Just before Frank ran away from his home he was after taking to drinking; and one night, and he coming into the house, after spending half the day in the tavern at the Cross, his father stepped out of his bedroom and himself and Frank had a terrible row altogether, and in the end, why, they struck one another and Jeremiah ordered his son to quit the house for ever.

So the next day, God help us, Frank went across the valley, to say farewell to his sweetheart, Eily

Kevane—she was a distant cousin of my father's people, so she was—and he asked Eily to be true to him during the years to come and he promised to send for her, or else come back again to marry her at home. And Eily promised to be true to Frank and they said goodbye to each other, and that same evening without as much as a farewell word to his father or his brother Stephen, Frank Mahony left his house. And just a year after that Jeremiah Mahony died: and then Stephen was all alone in the farmhouse.

Not as much as one line, or one word, Frank Mahony ever wrote to his brother from the time he was after leaving his home, imbeersa, and even Eily Kevane wasn't after getting a letter from him; and sometimes Stephen said to himself that his brother was surely dead and buried, and hardly a week passed by that Eily Kevane wasn't over at the farmhouse to know from Stephen if he had any tale or tidings of Frank.

And there was an idle, bad-minded, mischief-making sthronsha—Maure Barnane—living alongside of the tavern at the Cross; and, faith, Maure sent the story around the place that Eily Kevane was striving to coax Stephen Mahony to marry her and that she was running over, week after week, to his house, 'without a bit of shame in her,' thinking she'd come at the soft side of Stephen, some way or other, and twist a promise out of him, and then she'd hold him down to that!

Stephen Mahony was a harmless, good-natured, easy-going poor libe, and he only laughed at the story when he heard it first; but, faith, it turned out to be a serious matter enough for him later on, awonomsa fain; and so you'll say, when I'll tell you all about it.

A bad, gossiping, false-tongued woman, God forgive her, is enough to put a whole countryside of people at one another's throats, like the mad, wild beasts of the forest; and it wasn't Maure Barnane's fault, so it wasn't, that a black, unnatural murder didn't come to pass, and all on account of her lying, venomous tongue. . . This Maure Barnane had a sister married to a sailor in Cork city, and Maure went up to the city to spend a week with this sister, about two years or so after Jeremiah Mahony's death. And one evening, when Maure and her sister were walking in the city, who should they meet but Frank Mahony himself, and he after landing in Queenstown the very evening before. And Maure Barnane up and told him all about his father's death— 'twas the first he was after hearing about it, mind you— and after she easing her mind on that matter, why, didn't the melted vagabone of a woman speak of Eily Kevane, and didn't she hint at the same story about Eily and Stephen Mahony that she was after sending through the whole district before his face and he turned as pale as ashes.

And, 'I'll soon find out the truth of this for myself, so I will,' says he. 'I'll let 'em see,' says he, 'that I'm not a cursed fool between 'em!'

And not another word came out of his lips at that time, mossa; only he turned on his heel and passed down a side street, and Maure Barnane saw no more of him while she was in the city of Cork.

Back he went to his lodgings, where he was after spending the night before, and he pulled open his box, imbeersa, and out of a leather case inside of it didn't he take an elegant gold watch, that he was bringing home as a present for his brother Stephen, and he tossed it on the floor and ground it into bruss under his feet! And, after doing that, he pulled a gold locket out of another little leather case, and 'twas made in the shape of a true-lover's-knot, with a heart across the middle of it and the name 'Eily' across the middle of it in little, blue jewels, and, the Lord save us, he gave the same treatment to the locket that he was after giving to the gold watch, so he did, and then he put his heart's black, bitter curse on Eily and on his brother, if Maure Barnane's story really turned out to be the truth.

'And though I blame myself for not writing to Eily,' says he, and he talking to himself like a madman, 'still that's no excuse at all for her, if she's after breaking her solemn promise to me. 'Tis well she knew I'd stand to the share of the promise,' says he; 'and I didn't want to write to her till I could be sure of coming back to marry her—and then I said I'd give her a happy surprise instead, and not write any letter at all!'

And it chanced that the very next evening poor Eily Kevane ran across the valley to Stephen Mahony's house, to ask about Frank, as usual. Stephen was seated by the turf fire in the kitchen, reading a book, when Eily came in, while Cauth Moynihan, the servant woman was baking a bastable of bread in the chimney-corner. So Eily sat down by the fire, and after a few minutes the bread was baked and Cauth took it out of the bastable and put it standing up against the wall on the table over-right the fire, and then Cauth went up on the loft to fix the rooms and the beds before she'd come down to get Stephen's supper.

And no sooner was Cauth after leaving the kitchen when Eily Kevane took to shiver and to cry; 'Oh, Stephen, Stephen,' says she. 'I had a terrible dream last night about Frank. Sure, I thought he came into the kitchen here,' says she, 'and I was sitting where I'm sitting this minute, and his face was a pale as death and his two eyes blazing like coals in his head. And when I ran to welcome him,' says she, 'he struck down my hand with a cane he was holding in his fingers, and he cursed me and all belonging to me, and then he flung himself on you, Stephen,' says she, 'and I saw him drawing a long, rusty knife from his pocket—and with the terror of it all,' says she, 'I woke up then, and I was shivering from head to foot, and the coldness of death creeping over me, and my teeth knocking together in my head!'

And Stephen put his hand around Eily's neck, just as a fond brother might do, and he saying everything he could think of to console her; and at the very minute—God between us and harm—a footstep came to the kitchen door, and the door was roughly opened and Frank Mahony himself was standing before Stephen and Eily!

Glory be to God! You may say they got a shock, when they spotted him; and he never let on a bit as to his real suspicions—for now he felt almost sure that everything Maure Barnane was after telling him was the truth!—and he crossed over to the hearth and shook hands with Eily and with his brother, and he smiling a terrible smile, mossa, and his face like the face of a dead man. And the joyous words of welcome, God help us, died in poor Eily's throat, and not a word or syllable could she speak, why; so what could Frank Mahony think, I'm asking you, only that Maure Barnane's story was true? And when Eily stood up to go home at last Frank sat where he was, imbeersa, at the opposite side of the fire, and a black scowl across his features; and Stephen looked sideways at him, but he didn't like, you see, to say anything to him till Frank would be in a good humour again, and up Stephen jumps and says to Eily, and he trying to pass the thing off as a joke:

'Faith, I think I'll see you home myself Eily girl,' says he, 'as Frank seems to be too tired to leave the chimney-corner.'

And Frank never said a word, and Eily didn't know rightly what to say, and out the door with her, mossa, and Stephen Mahony at her heels,

And the minute the two of 'em were gone out Frank Mahony started up from his chair by the fire, and in his mad rage didn't he toss the chair across the hearth, with a crash that you'd hear all over the house; and down comes Cauth Moynihan from the loft, and when she spotted Frank and he standing on the hearth with his eyes blazing in his head, she let a screech of fright out of her, and she had the like to drop down in a dead faint on the floor.

And 'Glory be to God, Frank Mahony,' says she, 'and is it yourself that is in it, or is it your spirit?'

And I don't know what Frank Mahony said to her, but whatever it was Cauth Moynihan was mortal troubled in her mind, so she was.

And, 'Where's Stephen and Eily gone to, yerra?' says she. 'Sure, the two of 'em were here colloguing by the fire, and I going up on the loft to dress the beds.'

'Where would they be, Cauth?' says Frank Mahony, and his face as black as a winter night, why, 'only going across the valley together where they often go, by all accounts! And why wouldn't they?' says he, and he pretending to make little of it, the way Cauth Moynihan wouldn't have the laugh against him. 'Sure, Eily is Stephen's nearest neighbour, and 'tis only nice and civil to be friendly with your neighbours, and how could he let her face for home at this hour of the night without going with her for a bit of the way?' says he.

'Wisha, that's true for you, Frank boy,' says Cauth, and she suspecting nothing, awonomsa. 'Poor Eily often runs across the valley to us after her day's work is done.'

'Faith, so I can hear, Cauth,' says Frank, and he laughing—though at the same minute, the Lord save us, there were flames of mad jealousy and fury darting through his heart. 'And, sure, wouldn't it be a good plan,' says he, 'if Eily and Stephen made a match of it,' says he, and he looking under his eyes at Cauth Moynihan, 'before they stop.'

'But what about yourself and Eily, Frank boy?' says Cauth, and her eyes wide open with surprise. 'Is it the

way you're after changing your mind about her?' says
Cauth. 'And is that why you never wrote her one line, or
one word, all the time you were away?'

'I suppose 'twas something like that, Cauth,' says he,
and he looking away from her, and he saying it.

And divil another word came out of his lips on the
matter that night, though Cauth you may be sure, did all
she could to find out the real truth.

And as the days and the weeks went by, mossa, Frank
Mahony bided his time, and he watched and waited,
with a kind of smile on his face and hell's own black
bitterness down deep in his heart. Poor Stephen didn't
know what to make of his brother at all, at all,
awonomsa. He did all he could to be kind and civil and
brotherly to Frank, and to make him happy and content-
ed in the old family home; but somehow, he couldn't
come at the bottom of Frank's mind, good nor bad; and
as the two brothers sat at their meals together, or at the
fire, of a night, 'tis often Cauth Moynihan saw a terrible
look in Frank's eyes, and he staring at Stephen and poor
Stephen knowing nothing at all about it. God help us.
And Stephen couldn't but wonder, to be sure, why
Frank was so cool and distant to Eily Kevane, though he
couldn't bring himself to speak to Frank about it, and
Eily herself got shy and frightened, and 'twas seldom
now she ever came across the valley to the farmhouse.
But Stephen often met Eily, for all that, and the two of
'em always had a long talk together about Frank.

'I can't make him out at all, so I can't,' says poor Eily.
'I never saw a boy so changed, in all my life before! But
what can I do with him?' says she. ''Tain't my fault, anyway. So he must only see it out, I suppose, to the end.'

And it never flashed on Stephen's honest mind,
mossa, that Maura Barnane's lying stories could have
come to Frank's ears. He never cast a thought, at this
time, to Maure Barnane or to her whispers. Stephen

Mahony was so true and straight himself, mossa, that he couldn't be thinking of other people's roguery and divilment, only when some piece of villainy would be shoved under his very eyes, begannies, and he couldn't help but see it.

So a couple of months went by; and then Frank Mahony said to himself, one winter's evening, that he couldn't stand this any longer, why—that he wasn't a stick, or a stone, and that he'd let 'em all see it for themselves at last!

Right well he knew that Stephen and Eily used to meet constantly, ever since he returned home, although Eily was after boycotting the farmhouse the same as if she was in dread of catching some kind of a sickness, if she crossed the doorstep.

'Very well!' says Frank to himself, on this winter's evening. 'I'll put a stop to it all, on the mortal spot.'

And now 'tis worth your while to listen to me, so it is, for I'm coming to a strange part of my story.

Stephen Mahony was after leaving the farmhouse half an hour or so before this, and Frank was after seeing his brother take the road to the east.

'I'll meet him and he coming back,' says Frank, and he went up on the loft and opened his box and he took a long sailor's knife, with a horn handle, out of it, mossa, and shoved it into his pocket, and away with him into the darkness outside; and the wild winds and they screeching in fury all around him, and the angry rain and it beating on his burning cheeks. All that day he couldn't bring himself to speak to his brother Stephen: and now, God help us, the black rage of the murderer filled his heart.

And on he went, and he walking quicker and quicker; but there was no sign of Stephen, and Frank never knew how far he was after walking until, all of a sudden, why, he found himself at the gate of the old churchyard of

Toumpleen-Breedha, where his loved mother lay at rest. And something or other—God only knows what it was, mossa!—prompted him at that minute to go into the old churchyard and faith, so he did, and across the graves he went, in the wind and darkness, and the old trees and they lashing and groaning in the storm and the rain driving across his face. And he never stopped till he came to his mother's grave, under a hawthorn bush at the west side of the churchyard; and when he did reach it, glory be to God, there was some man lying on his face and hands across the grave, and he breaking his heart crying, why!

And Frank Mahony stooped down and caught the man by the shoulder and turned his face round to him, and if he did—praise be to God this night!—wasn't it his own brother Stephen that was in it, and the tears running down his cheeks like the rain. And when Frank saw that—and, sure, 'twas all the mercy of the good God, so it was!—he shoved his left hand into his pocket, and his right hand on his brother's shoulder all the time, and he pulled out the sailor's knife, and with all the strength of his arms he flung it from him into the briars and nettles at the lower end of the churchyard. And with that—glory be to God—something cracked inside in his heart (for he always loved his poor, dead mother, you see) and down he fell alongside of Stephen on the grave and tears of blood—or so they seemed to himself, mossa—tore their way up from his heart and out through his burning eyes.

And, 'Oh, mother, mother, mother,' says he, and he sobbing out loud, like a little child, ''twas you saved me this night from slaying my own brother!' says he—and with that he flung his arms round Stephen's neck and he clung to him and he crying mad, and he poured out his heart to Stephen and he told him all about Maure Barnane's lying story and all that was after passing

through his own distracted mind since then. . . So, through the mercy of God, everything was made clear as daylight between Frank and Stephen, and they kneeling by their mother's grave, that night in Toumpleen-Breedha.

And Stephen told Frank that he, himself came to their mother's grave that night to pray that Frank and himself might be the best of friends again, like old times. And then Stephen told Frank the full truth about poor Eily Kevane and that she was breaking her heart with sorrow over Frank's coldness towards her ever since he was after coming home. . .

So, to make a long story short, the end of it was, why, that Stephen Mahony made a fair division of the farm and helped Frank to build an elegant, fine dwelling-house on it: and Frank and Eily were married in the very next Shrove, God bless them!—and Stephen got a nice, tidy, slochter wife for himself too, before the same year was out.

So there's my story for you—word for word—the very way my poor mother often told it to me, and I a child long ago.

The Mystery of Ellen Maguire

I promised ye all last night that I had another queer story to tell you tonight; and, so I have, imbeersa. And I in my bed last night, I was thinking over it all, and the whole story came back to me again the same as if it happened only last week. And, when I fell asleep at last I was dreaming of poor Ellen Maguire, and I could hear her voice in my ears, as plain as if she was in bed with me, and she singing a song I often heard her singing long ago—a song that goes like this:

Come all ye maids, both fair and young,
That flourish in your prime, prime,
Be wise, beware! Keep your gardens clear,
And let no man steal your thyme, thyme,
  Let no man steal your thyme.

For when your thyme is all passed and gone,
No more they'll care for you, you.
There's not a place that your thyme grows waste.
But 'tis sprinkled over with rue, rue,
  'Tis sprinkled all over with rue.

And so on goes the song, and 'tis an elegant old song, so it is, and poor Ellen Maguire used to be a great warrant to sing it. God help us!

Mavrone! But 'tis little I thought, the first time I met Ellen Maguire, how the world was going to use the craythur, and what a strange history was before her, and she not to be able to escape from her allotment—no more than if she was tied to one of the rocks by the seashore, mossa, and the tide rushing in a-top of her, straight from the Atlantic itself!

The first time I ever laid eyes on Ellen Maguire was down in Rosscarbery, at Father John Power's tomb, one night, and she making 'the rounds' for a sick friend. There was a great crowd all around the tomb, and they saying the Rosary and praying other prayers, and some of them rubbing the dust off the tombstone to carry away for cures and one poor old woman, up to eighty years of age, and she lying flat on top of the tomb, God help us. And a terrible shower of rain came on about midnight, and I made room for Ellen Maguire alongside of myself under a bush, for shelter, and then the two of us began chatting, why, and my heart warmed to her from that minute. She was as fine a girl, so she was, as ever I laid my two eyes on in this world, imbeersa—with a grand, stately figure, and it as straight as a whip, and a head of shining yellow hair, all in ring-

31

lets, and skin the colour of the milk-white hawthorn blossom, with a rosy flush in each of her cheeks. And her two blue eyes were like jewels in her head, so they were, and as nice as she was to look at, why, she was ten times nicer in her ways and manner.

Molaire! The two of us got to be the greatest friends that night, I tell you; and, in the morning, before we parted, Ellen Maguire made me promise her that I'd stroll around to her home away west of Rosscarbery, near Glandore, in the following week some time; and, faith, so I did, and 'twas then I came to know her people.

Her father and mother and her sister, Kate, were living at the farmhouse at Droumbeg, and, sometimes, an aunt of Ellen's—a Mrs Donoghue, a widow-woman from Squince—used to come to Droumbeg to spend a week or two with Ellen's people.

The Widow Donoghue was a fine, jolly, warmhearted woman and she was cract alive about Ellen; and when she'd come to Droumbeg, Ellen would be hanging around her morning, noon and night, and where one would be the other would be. You might be sure of that, whatever! And Ellen's parents and her sister, Kate, were jealous of the Widow Donoghue being so great with Ellen and Ellen so fond of her!

And, 'You'll spoil Ellen, so you will, Aunt Mary,' Kate used to say sometimes to Mrs Donoghue, and other times Ellen's mother used to scold her sister-in-law for making so much of Ellen.

'Wisha, I'm half sorry I came here at all to Droumbeg,' the Widow Donoghue would say, when they'd all turn on her mind you! 'And only for Ellen, I'd never set my foot across your doorstep. She's the flower of the flock, so she is, God bless her!' Mrs Donoghue used to say. 'And there's no fear I'll do her any harm by being fond of her. If everyone is as true to Ellen as I am, she'll be one of the luckiest and happiest girls in all the County Cork.'

And when she'd talk this way, mossa, you'd think the others wouldn't be a bit too well pleased, why; and they'd throw jealous eyes on Ellen and her Aunt Mary. And, little by little, this kind of feeling grew worse and worse, until, in the end, the Widow Donoghue used to be half afraid to come visiting at Droumbeg at all, at all.

Ellen's mother was very big in herself and Kate took after her in that way, but Ellen was more like her father's people, the Maguires; and Ellen's father, John Maguire, would be all right only for his wife, imbeersa; but, for peace sake, I suppose, he had to give in to her and to humour her grand notions and listen to her raw-maysh about her big relations and her rich uncle out in California. She was never done talking about this uncle and his property and his carriages, why!

'And he'll never marry—I'm sure of that,' she used to say, 'and he'll leave all his money and his property to us, whenever he dies. And, I'm not wishing Uncle Jer to die when I talk like that,' she used to say; 'but, he's an old man, and it ain't likely he can live many years long!'

'There'll be no standing Mag at all, at all, if her Uncle Jer dies and leaves her his money,' the Widow Donoghue said to me one evening—the second visit I paid to Droumbeg. 'In some way,' says she, ''twould be better for herself if she never got it. To tell you the truth, Kitty,' says she, 'I'm half in dread of her, so I am! She's always finding fault with me and blaming me for being so taken up with my niece, Ellen. But I wouldn't give Ellen's little finger,' says she, 'for twenty women like her mother or her sister, Kate. And I'm ashamed of my brother, John, so I am, to be under their thumb the way he is. He's no man,' says Widow Donoghue, 'to let his wife and his daughter ride over him and order him about!'

And this was true enough, mossa—every word of it
—but, 'twas no good to be talking. As long as Ellen's
mother and Kate were in the house at Droumbeg they'd
try to master everyone else under the roof, so they
would; that was one thing certain, awonomsa!

And, one day, in the end of the harvest, what do you
think, but, didn't the news reach Ellen's mother that her
Uncle Jer was after dying suddenly out in California;
and, faith, if it did, Mrs Maguire made up her mind to
start off, with her husband and her daughter, Kate, to
see after her uncle's property herself.

'If we trust to the lawyers, John,' says she to her
husband, 'they'll only make ducks and drakes of the
property—and, maybe, do me out of it altogether in the
end! The only sure plan,' says she, 'is for me to be on the
spot myself, to see that the terms of Uncle Jer's will are
carried out honestly; and the sooner we make a start the
better,' says she. 'Delays are dangerous!'

So, I needn't tell you, I suppose, her husband was said
by her; and the Widow Donoghue was sent for to
Squince to come over quick to Droumbeg, to keep Ellen
company and help to look after the place, until the rest
of the family came back from America.

And, faith, Mrs Donoghue was only too glad to come,
imbeersa, particularly when Mrs Maguire and Kate
were not to be under the roof with her; and the very day
after the widow-woman arrived from Squince, John
Maguire and his wife and Kate started for Queenstown.

And, faith, I never knew a bit about the business,
good nor bad, for a week after, and I happened to be
going down the boreen to the farmhouse at Droumbeg,
one evening in the first week of September, and I heard
Ellen within in the dairy and she singing out loud like a
skylark.

And, 'Glory be to goodness!' says I to myself. 'What's
on her at all and she to be singing like that? It must be

the way,' says I, 'that her mother and Kate are gone into town or something!'

And, molaire, when I went into the dairy and Ellen up and told me her news, you may say I wasn't sorry to hear it!

'Wisha, fair weather after them and snow to their heels, Ellen, alaylum,' says I to her—'ay, if they were your mother and father and sister itself!'

And in came the Widow Donoghue with a pail of milk on her head and I saying the words, and 'Amen to that, Kitty,' says she. 'Amen to that! And, would you believe it, Kitty woman,' says she, 'the house ain't the same since they started for America. Sure, all my old friends and neighbours are after coming to see me during the week,' says she—'people that never crossed the door-step, some of them since my brother John was married.

'And by the same token, Kitty,' says she, 'we're giving a party on next Wednesday night, and you'll have to wait for it, so you will—ay, and to take your own part, too,' says she, 'in the singing and dancing that night.'

And sure, I suppose I needn't tell you I was only too glad to stay on at Droumbeg till the night of the dance; and 'twas one of the best nights I ever had, so it was, in my travels. I'm sure there was up to forty people in the house that night and, when they'd be tired out from dancing, they'd start to sing like mad—some of the finest songs you could hear anywhere, imbeersa! But, the best singer in the house that night was a play-actor man—of the name of Paul Carew. Sure I never could forget his name, nor himself, ayther, begannies.

How he happened to come to Droumbeg that night was this way. . . He was after having some sort of a row with the other play-actors of the company, and when their time was up in Skibbereen (they were there for a week in the Town Hall) Paul Carew left them, and out to Glandore he came to spend a few days by the seaside;

and, if he did, he picked up with some of the folks around, and one of them coaxed him to come over to Droumbeg that night of the dance for a bit of jolification, why!

And, molaire, Paul Carew was the life and soul of the house that night, so he was—a fine, tall, elegant young man, not a day older than thirty and he having a grand curly head of black hair, and long features and two bright black eyes, full of drollery, and his teeth like a row of beads in his head, they were so white and even.

And, faith, he wasn't long in the house that night when he picked up with Ellen Maguire and took her out to dance the Highland shottische with him; and, if you travelled Ireland, why, you wouldn't see such a handsome pair as the two of them and they skipping round together in the dance, and old Seamus Rue and he playing *Munnymusk* on his fiddle, within the chimney corner. And, from that out till morning, Ellen Maguire and Paul Carew never parted company; and when he'd be singing a song, Ellen would join in the chorus and when she'd start one of her own, he wouldn't delay long to strike in with her, begannies, and you couldn't tell which of them was best.

'Awonomsa fain,' says the Widow Donoghue in a whisper to me and Ellen and Paul Carew singing *Shule Agra* together, ''tis a pity them two wouldn't be ever and always in each other's company, so it is. Faith, Kitty,' says she, and she laughing and taking a pinch of snuff for herself, 'you'd think 'twas made for one another the two of them are! I'm in dread we'll never again be able to part them!'

And, 'twas half in joke she said it, but, mavrone, we soon found out 'twas no joke at all, why! For, after that night of the spree, Paul Carew and Ellen were together, day by day, and 'twas no good for anyone to try and come between them.

For the first week or so Ellen's aunt thought 'twas a bit of harmless fun, between Ellen and Paul Carew; but, 'twasn't long till the neighbours began to carry stories to the Widow Donoghue and soon the news went like wild-fire all over the place.

Sure, myself heard it from two or three people, one market day, in Rosscarbery, how Paul Carew and Ellen Maguire were going to make a match of it on the mortal spot and the marriage was to take place in a week's time or so. And, as quick as I could leg it, on with me south to Droumbeg, and just and I going down the boreen to the farmhouse, didn't I hear Ellen and she singing *Cush na Breedha* and there I spotted her sitting on the mossy ditch on the Paurkeen Bwee all by herself.

And, 'Wisha, God save you, Ellen, alay,' says I to her; 'and tell me is this the truth I'm after hearing today about yourself and Paul Carew?' says I, 'or is it a lie the neighbours are fixing on you or what?'

And every drop of blood in her body rushed into her two cheeks, you'd think, and I asking her the question; and she didn't deny it at all, but she told me Paul Carew was after asking her to marry him.

'He's the only one I ever met that I'd be satisfied to marry,' says she. 'From the first minute I laid eyes on him my heart lepped out to him,' says she and a kind of shiver going through her from head to foot. 'And I'd be satisfied to beg the world, Kitty, and to live on a meal a day,' says she, 'only to be alongside of him always and to hear his voice in my ears and to feel his hand holding mine,' says she, 'and to be able to take my fill of looking at him any time I'd like.'

'Wisha, God direct you, Ellen Maguire!' says I to her, and, begannies, I didn't right know what to say, so I didn't. 'And, tell me, Ellen, alay,' says I, 'does your Aunt Mary know about it at all?'

'To be sure, she knows about it, Kitty,' says Ellen.

'Sure, hasn't she eyes in her head to see it all for her-self?' says she. 'But she wants me to wait till my father and mother and Kate are home from California. She's in dread of her life to let it go ahead and they to be so far away,' says she.

And, while she was talking who should come up the boreen to the pair of us only the Widow Donoghue her-self, and she took to clap her hands and shed tears when she spotted me.

And, 'Oh, Kitty woman,' says she, and the tears run-ning down her cheeks, 'ain't this a nice turn for Ellen there to give me, and I so fond of her ever and always,' says she, 'to go and pick up with a play-acting man, and he not to have a pound in his pocket, I suppose,' says she, 'and to insist on marrying him and her father and mother and sister, Kate, at the other end of the world,' says she. 'And, sure, if I let her have her own way, I'd never hear the end of it,' says she. 'I might as well run out of the country and never show my face to her people again in this world.'

'I told you before, Aunt Mary,' says Ellen to her, 'that I'll take all the blame on my own shoulders so I will. I'll tell them you did your best to put a stop to my marriage. But it can't be put a stop to,' says Ellen, and 'twas easy enough to see she meant every word she was saying. 'And, if I was to do your bidding, Aunt Mary, and to wait till they'd be home from California, I might make up my mind,' says she, 'to say goodbye to Paul Carew for ever; for 'tis well I know,' says she, 'they'd never give their consent to anything like it. But I can't give him up,' says she. 'If anything parted me from him now I'd go out of my mind,' says she. 'I'd kill myself!—for I couldn't live without him.'

And, to make a long story short, why, didn't Ellen Maguire carry out her plans, in spite of her Aunt Mary. 'Twas no good for anyone to try and stop her; and, in the end, the Widow Donoghue made up her mind to let the marriage go on, begannies, no matter how things would be afterwards. 'And, sure , if all comes to all, Kitty,' said the poor craythur of a woman to me, 'haven't I enough for the three of us?—for Ellen and Paul and myself? I'm satisfied to let them come and live with me west at Squince, if they can't manage to keep a home of their own, why. Or Ellen can make her home with me,' says she, 'till Paul is able to provide a home for her later on.'

And, mossa, 'twas settled this way, and the day of the wedding was fixed and the Widow Donoghue was in dread of her life to write a line out to California to tell Ellen's people about it. 'They'll find out time enough,' says she, 'for themselves!'

And Ellen was as happy as the day was long, the poor girl, and Paul Carew and herself were always together, singing and chatting and laughing, like two children, God help us!

And so the days passed away until it only wanted two days of the marriage. 'Twas to be a private wedding, without any spree or dance or anything of that sort, good nor bad, why; and I didn't like to be staying on at the house, and they all so busy, so I made up my mind to leave Droumbeg and to go west to Castlehaven that same evening.

Poor Ellen wanted to keep me, in spite of me; but I had my own way, begannies—and sorry I was afterwards I didn't stay with her!

But, we never know how things are to turn out in this world, God help us. When we rise in the morning how can we tell what's to happen before the night falls again. Laughing we are at one time of the day and crying the next. We are like people that would be blindfolded, as we go along—just trusting to chance, or to God, to keep us out of trouble and danger!

And, maybe, 'tis all the best, too, to have it like that.

What's the use of looking for trouble coming towards us, like a black cloud? Whenever it comes 'twill be too soon, why? Time enough to bid the divil good morra when you meet him.

So, away with me west under the hill from Droumbeg, that same evening; and, faith, I wasn't a quarter of a mile on my journey and I crossing a ridge of heath and rahanagh just above the Druid's Circle, when I spotted Paul Carew himself and he standing in a gap just below me, and he reading a letter and his face the colour of chalk and his two eyes starting out of his head, why?

And I drew in behind a furze bush to watch him, so I did—and, wirrasthrue, wirrasthrue, but something whispered to me that there was bad work going on!

After he reading the letter, mind you, didn't he take a kind of a mad fit and didn't he tear it up into fifty pieces and scatter it right and left; and then he flung his two hands across his temples and let out a groan out of him and a weakness passed over me and I listening to him. And, after that he rubbed his handkerchief across his forehead and up the hill he came, as quick as lightning, and he passed me out, two yards from the furze bush I was under, and he never spotted me, imbeersa, and away with him, straight for Droumbeg.

And, faith, I delayed no longer, so I didn't, but I struck for the road at once and I never stopped walking till I landed in Castlehaven, to a house I used to stop in whenever I travelled that way.

And, for a week or so after that, I never heard a word about Ellen Maguire or her marriage; and, one evening, and I walking along the road near Rineen, didn't I meet with the Widow Donoghue herself, driving in a jennet's car, and she on her way home to Droumbeg from the Skibbereen market.

And, the instant minute she spotted me she got as pale as death, so she did, and she pulled up the jennet and asked me to get into the car and go back with her to Droumbeg for the night. I knew well enough there was some trouble on her, God help her; so, into the car with me, and I never asked her a question till we were out of the village of Rineen.

And, 'Wisha, ma'am,' says I to her then, 'what's on you at all, at all? Is it the way you're fretting after Ellen or what?'

And, with that she began to cry, and be in a fit, the Lord between us and harm this night!

And, 'Oh, Kitty, Kitty,' says she. 'Sure, Ellen ran away from Droumbeg and never waited at all for her wedding day. Herself and Paul Carew,' says she, 'eloped together two days before the marriage. 'Twas the very night,' says she, 'you went west to Castle-haven.'

And she up and told me the story, and she killing herself crying all the time; and, as well as I could make it out from her, 'twas this way it happened.

Ellen threw on her shawl and went up the boreen as usual, to meet Paul Carew that evening, why; but she never returned to the farmhouse. And, on the next morning, a little boy ran into the cowhouse to the Widow Donoghue, with a letter from Ellen to say she was after eloping with Paul Carew and promising she'd write full particulars as to their marriage later on.

'And, glory be to goodness,' says I, 'did she go without her clothes and all the things she had ready?' says I. 'Do you mean to tell me, ma'am, she carried nothing only what she had on her back?'

'Maybe, she'd send for her clothes after a bit, Kitty,' says the Widow Donoghue, as well as she could speak with the dint of trouble.

'Mavrone, mavrone, but I'm in dread 'twas the unlucky marriage for poor Ellen!' says I; and I up and told her all I was after spotting and I hiding under the furze bush the evening I left Droumbeg.

'And, I'm as sure as I'm alive, ma'am,' says I, 'that 'twas the way Paul Carew got some bad news in the letter he was reading—and this was the whole cause,' says I, 'of the elopement between poor Ellen and himself that night!'

And, 'Time will tell, Kitty—time will tell, why!' was all the Widow Donoghue could say, in answer to me, and the words, you'd think, had like to choke her and she saying them.

And, begannies, the days and weeks went by and no tale or tidings ever came as to Ellen and Paul Carew and Christmas came and passed, and then, the Widow Donoghue got a letter from Ellen's father from California, to say they were all starting for home at last, full up of money, after selling out the big property that was left for them by his wife's rich uncle in Los Angeles.

'And, we're going to buy Carrigmore and settle Kate in it with her husband,' the letter went on. 'She's after picking up a fine, handsome young man—a native of County Tipperary—out here, and he's travelling home with us to Ireland. 'But, Droumbeg won't suit us now, Mary. Carrigmore is just the place we want.' Carrigmore was an old-fashioned rambling mansion, about half a mile to the south of Droumbeg. It once belonged to the Barry family; but 'twas empty for years and a caretaker was looking after it—Dannie Flur, a distant cousin of the Maguires. And when the Widow Donoghue read this in the letter, she got the colour of death, and I thought she was going to drop down fainting on the floor.

And, 'What mad notion is this they're after taking?' says she and she hardly able to speak. 'Carrigmore is no place for them. 'Tis an unlucky, haunted house. Sure, everyone knows things are seen there,' says she, 'and 'tis as much as Dannie Flur can do to stop in it at all, at all,

God help us!'

'Wisha, I suppose, ma'am, they're ready to risk their lives for the grandeur of living in a gentleman's house,' says I, bitter enough; 'so, you may's well let them have their own way,' says I, 'and, if they suffer for it, 'tis all their own fault, ma'am, and not yours,' says I. 'So they can't blame you, whether or which.'

But she only shook her head and wouldn't be said by me, right or wrong.

And, 'No, no!' says she, 'whatever happens, they mustn't go to live in Carrigmore. I'll see to that whatever!'

And, a week afterwards, back they came—John Maguire and his wife and Kate—and they dressed out in the grandest style, in silks and feathers and ear rings and brooches, mossa, and an elegant overcoat on John Maguire and it trimmed with fur, and two big trunks with them that could hardly come in at the door at Droumbeg.

And Frank O'Meara, Kate's sweetheart, was to come after them in a week or so, they said. He was after going home to see his own people near Nenagh.

And when the Widow Donoghue told them all about Ellen's runaway marriage, it had like to drive them distracted, why!

'And, 'tis well I knew,' says Ellen's mother, 'no good luck would follow her and to be in your hands, Mary Donoghue! Bad advice and bad training is all you ever gave her,' says she. 'And here's the wind-up of it all.'

A regular pilimaloo was ruz at Droumbeg over the elopement by Ellen's people—and only for being in a hurry to see about the purchase of Carrigmore and fitting up the old place before Frank O'Meara was back from Tipperary, matters would be twice as bad.

'Twas all no use for the Widow Donoghue to try and stop them from going to live at Carrigmore. She might as well be talking to the wild winds to strive to keep them from blowing. And John Maguire got possession of Carrigmore in the following week and after furnishing a few rooms in one of the wings of the ancient mansion, the family moved into it a few days later. And, molaire, that was the unlucky moving, so it was! The very first night they spent under the haunted roof of Carrigmore, wasn't Kate nearly frightened out of her life, mossa, by what she heard in the dead hour of the night from the locked-up deserted wing of the old mansion. She couldn't settle herself to sleep that night, it seemed, and up she got about midnight and down to the kitchen with her for a drink of milk, thinking it would make her heavy in herself, you see, and put her to sleep after. And, the Lord save us, and she going back to her room and she passing the locked door, shutting off the back rooms to themselves, why, didn't she hear someone running about one of the rooms beyond the door, and then someone burst out laughing, and then a terrible screech came, and away with Kate back to her room and the cold sweat streaming over her face like the rain.

And, sure, the same thing happened many a night after that, and even in the daytime, they'd hear footsteps beyond the locked door; and Dannie Flur thought to persuade them, why, 'twas rats or bats were inside in the rooms, and he was after losing the key and couldn't open the door, he said, but Kate and her mother and even John Maguire himself, were half out of their minds with fright, awonomsa!

And, 'It must be true what the people around always said about Carrigmore,' says John Maguire to his sister, the Widow Donoghue, one day, he met her in Skibbereen. (She was after leaving Droumbeg, at this time, you see, and going home to her own place at Squince.) 'The house is haunted, Mary, sure enough; and only we're expecting Frank O'Meara to come to stay a week with us before Kate's marriage,' says he, 'we'd leave the place on the mortal spot and go back to the Droumbeg farmhouse.'

'And you'd do right, John, to do that,' says the Widow Donoghue, and she shaking all over and she saying it. 'Didn't I warn ye all not to go to that cursed house? But no,' says she, 'ye wouldn't be said by me —not me! 'Twas the way you wanted to brag and boast and show off before the neighbours and let them all see ye had money enough to settle down in a gentleman's house and place,' says she. 'And the divil mend ye all,' says she, and she losing her temper, why! 'That's all the pity I have for ye, and to be the way ye are, through your own folly and nonsense!'

And, the very next day, didn't Frank O'Meara come to Carrigmore; and I got a good look at him, and he driving down by Roury; for 'twas by Clonakilty and Rosscarbery he came. A fine, good-looking young man he was, surely, tall and straight and well-dressed, began-nies, and I couldn't help thinking of poor Ellen, and he passing me on the car, and I was saying to myself, God help us, what a handsomer, kinder wife she'd make for him than Kate only for her unfortunate marriage. Mavrone, I was always thinking of her and wondering what was after happening her at all, at all.

But, here's my story for ye—an now I want ye all to listen to me, because I'm coming to the queerest part of it, and there's not much more to tell.

On the very first night Frank O'Meara spent at Carrigmore the whole house was upset in the dead of night, with wild screeches from the locked-up wing, and things pelted hither and over, and doors banged, until you'd think a whole band of robbers were after breaking into the house, why?

And up jumps John Maguire in the middle of all the

pilimaloo, and he shouted to Dannie Flur to rise at once, and so he did, begannies, and 'twasn't long till Frank O'Meara joined them and Kate and her mother and the servant girl, Hannie Caydhogawn, and they all shivering with fright.

And, 'Dannie Flur,' says John Maguire, ''taint a bit of good for you to be telling me 'tis the way you're after losing the key of that locked door. I asked you twice already,' says John, 'ayther to unlock the door or to break it open. Now I'll wait on you no longer.'

'Frank,' says he, and he catching a hold of Kate's sweetheart by the shoulder and he holding a lantern in the other hand, 'help me, like a good man, to burst in the locked door,' says he. ''Tis the only way to find out the cause of this mystery.'

And, awonomsa fain, the two men made a charge at the door and Mrs Maguire and Kate and Hannie Caydhogawn, and the teeth chattering in their heads, and Dannie Flur as pale as paper; and, with one drive of his shoulder, didn't my brave Frank O'Meara drive in the door in splinters, and John dashed in over the rubbish, and the lantern held high up over his head; and, God bless the hearers, who do you think they found inside in one of the rooms and she after smashing everything all around her and her face and hands streaming with blood, why?

Who, but poor Ellen Maguire herself—no other—as true as I'm telling you the story this night!

And, after they securing her with ropes and locking her up in another room, didn't Dannie Flur up and tell them all about it. And, sure, 'twas simple enough when the whole story was told, why? But, you'd never guess it —never—and I couldn't believe it first, when I heard it, good nor bad.

'Twas the way poor Ellen, that evening she went to meet Paul Carew—the very evening I left Droumbeg for

Castlehaven—'twas the way she met Paul on the hillside west of the farmhouse, and he up and told her he was after getting a letter from his lawful wife, that he thought was dead and buried eighteen months before that, and he didn't know what in the world to do!

And, when poor Ellen heard this terrible piece of news, faith, her brain wasn't able to stand it and she went astray on the very spot. And, while she was screeching and tearing her hair, up comes her Aunt Mary, the Widow Donoghue, and Dannie Flur, with her (he happened to be over at Droumbeg that night, about a sick colt) and Dannie and Paul caught a hold of Ellen and held her between them, and then the Widow Donoghue, in her fright of Ellen's parents hearing the news, thought of a plan to keep the whole truth a secret from everyone.

And, 'For God's sake, Dannie,' says she, 'hide her away in one of the old rooms at Carrigmore and keep her under lock and key, and I'll let on to her people 'twas the way she eloped with Paul Carew—and I'll tell the same story to all the neighbours. Maybe she'd get better after a few days,' said she; 'and then we can think of some other plan.'

And, faith, Dannie Flur did what she asked him, and Paul Carew left the place that night, and poor Ellen was locked up at Carrigmore, sure enough. But she never got back her senses, God help us, until the very night before she died in the Cork hospital where her heart-broken father took her the morning after they found out the truth. And when her mind got clear, imbeersa, the poor unfortunate girl told her story to her father, just as I'm after telling it to you; and, a few hours later she was no more.

And, after that, the family tried to hush up the story, as well as they could, and the Widow Donoghue, one day, I met her in Skibbereen, warned me, for my life, to keep a still tongue in my head about the whole unlucky business. And, so I did, begannies—and the story never passed my lips till tonight. And it happened, years and years ago, and Kate Maguire and Frank O'Meara went back to America after their marriage and John Maguire and his wife sold out Droumbeg and settled down in a small house in Cork city after that.

The Warning

I told ye last night, mossa, that I'd have a story for you tonight to give you a good laugh, why!

And, begannies, and I knitting a stocking today, and I sitting all by myself on the big flat stone down by the edge of the lake, didn't every bit of the old story come back to my mind, imbeersa, the same as if someone was whispering into my ear—though 'tis many a long day, so it is, since it happened.

And, sure, I couldn't but begin to laugh to myself, and I thinking over it; and I never knew a bit till I heard Norrie Bwee, and she passing west with some groceries that she was after buying over at Kit Collins's, and 'What the divil are you laughing at like that, Kitty?' says Norrie. 'Or is it the way you're getting light in the head or what?'

And, sure, no wonder, she'd say it, awonomsa fain!

But here's my story for you now, and let ye all gather close to the blazing fire till you hear it, and ye needn't be in dread I'll tell ye anything that will frighten the heart out of ye tonight, whatever!. . .

I was staying for a few days with the Hegarty family, a few miles to the south-west of Bantry, at the time of the beginning of my story, why, and one fine September evening myself and Nano Hegarty, the eldest girl of the house, set out from her home to have a bit of fun for our-selves with some friends of ours in the town, mossa; for 'twas a fair day in Bantry, and a lot of the people weren't after going home as yet.

Faith, 'tain't like that now, awonomsa! Sure, if you were to go into the towns after four or five o'clock in the evening, on the fair days that's in it with the last few years, the divil a one you'd see, good nor bad, if 'twouldn't be a handful of men, here and there, and they stuck in the public houses and they drinking.

But, at the time I'm telling you about, 'twas different, so it was; and maybe for half the night after the fair the streets and the houses would be full up of jolly people and they all singing and dancing and telling funny yarns to one another, why, and fiddlers and ballad singers and Trick o' the Loops; and 'twould do your heart good, so it would, to be among 'em!

And, 'For God's sake, hurry on, Kitty, you divil, or we'll lose half the sport!' says Nano Hegarty.

And an elegant girl she was, faith, from the top of her head to the sole of her foot, imbeersa, and 'twas no wonder to me that all the boys were mad about poor Nano; for the flash of her blue eyes and the smile of her red lips and the dimples in her pink cheeks and the soft, melting tones of her voice, why, would coax the very birds off of the bushes.

And, faith, we were only just going into the town when we met a fine, decent, well dressed young man, and he riding out, and a woman in a hood-cloak and she upon a pillion behind him, on the horse's back.

And 'twas well I knew the pair of 'em—Dan Herlihy from Coomhola, and his mother—for 'twas no secret to me, begannies, that Dan Herlihy was out of his mind, why, with the dint of love for Nano Hegarty!

But, some way or other, Nano wouldn't give in, good nor bad, whenever I'd tell her she was fond of Dan in her heart.

She'd only toss her head and maybe she'd tell me sometimes to mind my own business and not to be tormenting her, mossa—and I knowing all the time, she was just as fond of the poor chap as he was of her, if only she'd look into her own heart, why, and open her two eyes to the truth!

And, begannies, 'tis many a young colleen oge I'm after meeting in my rambles that's suffering from the same complaint as Nano was that evening. With the dint of divilment, or something else, awonomsa, they won't give in that they'd be caught and landed by any man alive—they're so mighty cute and big in themselves, moryeh! And, the Lord knows, half of 'em don't deserve to get a good man at all—the whipsters!—only to be left in the lurch in the end.

But, mind you, I'm not saying one word against Nano Hegarty, when I say all this, mossa. She was never proud or stand-off with Dan Herlihy; only she used to say Dan was too much in earnest whenever he'd meet her, and, 'Faith, 'tis time enough for me to be thinking of settling down like my mother,' Nano used to say, 'when I'm after having a bit of fun and jollification out of the world first!'

So when Dan Herlihy wanted to put some soft talk on her this evening—and he having a sup of drink inside of his skin, though he wasn't what you'd call fond of drink, good nor bad, mind you!—Nano pulled away from him, in a minute, or two, and, 'If you're coming any further with me, Kitty woman,' says she to me, 'you'd better come along, why! 'Tis too late in the evening now for romancing!' says she, and she throwing an arch look at Dan and his mother over her shoulder, and she saying it.

'Wisha, the Lord direct that girl!' says Dan's mother to me, and Nano and she whisking away along the road into the town, and she pulling her shawl about her.

'Amen, ma'am!' says myself sharp enough, why; because there's no fear I'd listen to a joking word from anyone behind Nano's back; and away with me after Nano, and I not waiting for any more talk out of Ellen Herlihy.

And, begannies, we weren't ten minutes in the town, mossa, when we heard an elegant fiddler and he playing *The Cork Hornpipe* at the corner of the street, and two country lads and they dancing for him, and a whole crowd of people and they standing all around in a ring. And down with the two of us, imbeersa—Nano and myself—and 'twasn't long till we joined in the crowd molaire! If we did, 'twas worth our while, so it was, to see the dancers and to listen to the music, why! You'd think the fiddler was driving sparks of fire out of the fiddle, he put such spirit into the tune: and as good a warrant as he was to play, the two boys were a match for him and they dancing.

And after a bit, faith, I took notice of a tall, black-haired, good-looking boy, and he standing in the crowd, just close to us, and his two black eyes and they lepping out of his head, mossa, and they fastened on Nano's face: and, somehow, I didn't like the way he was looking at Nano, and I whispered a few words in her ear; and, with that, Nano threw a sharp look at the black-haired boy; but the divil a fear he put any heed to her sharp look, why, only to keep staring her straight in the face.

'Well, of all the daring rascals ever I met, that boy is one of the foremost,' says I to Nano, and I saying it out loud on purpose, and the way he'd hear me.

And what do you think, mind you, didn't he only laugh and grin at me, and he making a right mock of me before the people near us; and I was just going to pull Nano away and to go to the opposite side of the fiddler, when who should come up to us only Mary Kate Lynch and her brother Stephen, old school companions of

Nano's that she knew all her life, mossa. The Lynch's farmhouse was about two miles from Nano's, close to the road to Glengariffe.

And, faith, I didn't think any more about the black-haired boy, and Mary Kate and Stephen and they putting talk on myself and Nano—for they were a real lighthearted, airy pair, the two of 'em, God bless 'em!—and the four of us stood laughing and chatting, and we saying everything that came into our heads, why, and 'twasn't long till Mary Kate invited Nano to go to their own house on the next Sunday evening for certain.

'We're expecting some friends of ours from Durrus,' says Mary Kate. 'And we'll knock up a bit of a dance,' says she. 'So be sure to come on Sunday evening about seven o'clock, Nano,' says Mary Kate. 'And maybe you'd like to come, too, Kitty,' says she, and she turning to myself, the craythur.

'Oh, wisha,' says I. 'God knows how far away I'd be from here on Sunday evening, girl dear!' says I. 'But, I'm thankful to you, all the same, Mary Kate,' says I, 'and maybe I'd go to see you some other time before long.'

And just and I saying it, mossa, didn't I spot the black-haired boy again, and he shoving a bit nearer to us, if you please, and his two mad, black eyes and they fixed on Nano's face.

'And for God's sake, Mary Kate,' says I, in a whisper, 'who's that boy over there?' says I—'the lad with the navy-blue suit and the posy stuck in his button-hole, and the black eyes and moustache?' says I. 'Whoever the divil he is,' says I, I don't like the look of him, some-how!'

And Mary Kate threw her eyes on the black-haired laddo, and says she to me; 'Yerra, sure,' says she, 'ain't he Jer Callanan, the Widow Callanan's son, from Tubberbeg—a prime joker, ever inch of him,' says she.

'Come let us get away out of this, Kitty,' says she, 'the four of us, before that scamp puts any of his lingo on us,' says Mary Kate.

And, begannies, we took her advice, so we did, and we saw no more of Jer Callanan for the rest of the evening, thanks be to God.

And, faith, we had a few jolly hours of it, in Bantry, and after we leaving Mary Kate and Stephen we fell in with some of Nano's neighbours, and we were all home together, so we were, in high good humour, about nine o'clock.

And, sure, I fully intended to strike for the road a day or two after, mossa; but I caught some kind of a slydhawn, why, and Nano's mother wouldn't hear of me leaving the house till I was as well as ever again, the craythur. And when the Sunday came round I was well enough, thank God, to go to last Mass in Bantry, myself and Nano; and the two of us were sitting together in the back of the long car, and the servant-boy and he driving us home after Mass, when, all of a sudden, Nano shoved nearer to me, and says she, and she whispering in my ear.

'Yerra, Kitty,' says she, 'didn't I see Jer Callanan in the chapel,' says she, 'and he watching me the same as a cat would watch a mouse,' says she. 'I wouldn't like that boy, good nor bad,' says she. 'And I'll go to first Mass every other Sunday,' says she, 'with God's help.'

'Faith, I'm sorry I didn't see him today, Nano girl!' says I, 'because if I did, I'd give him a look that would be as good as a process! . . . But don't be troubling your head about him, alay machree,' says I to her, and I striving to cheer her up. 'You'll have a good night tonight with the Lynchs, so you will, and I hope you'll enjoy it, Nano!'

But you may say 'twas surprised I was when Nano shook her head, mossa, and a kind of frightened look came into her two eyes, and she shoving nearer to me.

'I didn't like to say anything about it, Kitty,' says she; 'but I had a queer dream last night, so I had,' says she. 'I thought I was on my way to the Lynch's house, and I on the old mountain road near the Lis; and all of sudden,' says she, 'didn't my poor sister that's dead run out from behind a furze-bush right before me,' says she, 'and she held up her hand,' says she, 'and I looking into her face, and I never thought she was dead at all,' says poor Nano, 'she looked so like what she used to be, God rest her soul. . .'

'Sure, poor Mollie was always cract about me, Kitty,' says she, 'and I thought I couldn't live a week after her death! . . . And now and she standing before me on the mountain road just below the Lis,' says Nano, 'you may say I felt overjoyed to see her! But a terrible sad look came into her eyes, Kitty, and she lifting up her hand, as if to warn me not to go another step on my road, and "Turn back, Nano, for the love of God," says she, "and go home for yourself, and if you don't be said by me," says she, "you'll come to troubles and misfortune."'

'And I woke up then, Kitty, and I didn't stop crying for a full hour after that,' says Nano; 'and I'm after making up my mind,' says she, 'not to go to the Lynchs at all tonight.'

'Wisha, maybe 'twould be as lucky for you not, girl dear,' says I to Nano. 'Sure after that dream, mossa, 'twould be like flying in the face of Providence, for you to venture!'

'Nothing would make me venture,' says she, 'after such a warning as that; so I'm going to ask you to ramble west to the Lynch's house this evening, Kitty, and tell 'em not to be expecting me,' says she. 'And then my mind will be at ease.'

So this was fixed on, why; and sure myself was only too glad to ramble west to the Lynch's, because I was always fond of the family, and so I ought, awonomsa fain!

And just about nightfall, I threw a shawl of Nano's over my head and shoulders—'twas a newer shawl than my own, and poor Nano forced me to put it on me—and away with me along the mountain road and I tuning to myself, and I thinking of the pleasant night that was before me.

And now 'tis worth your while to listen to me, so it is!

'Twas nearly dark, mossa, by the time I came to the bend of the road just below the Lis—the very spot, God bless the hearers, where Nano saw her poor sister's spirit, in the dream—and at that very minute and I going round the corner of the road, as true as I'm telling you my story, didn't I see a jennet's car and it pulled up by the side of the road and a young boy (as well as I could make out in the darkness) and he holding the jennet by the head.

And before I had time to say one word, mossa, didn't I hear a sharp little whistle just alongside of me, and out jumped a tall young man from the bushes at the side of the road, and he having a long overcoat down to his heels. And, 'You're welcome, Nano Hegarty,' says he. 'I'm waiting for you since nightfall. I heard you telling Mary Kate Lynch you'd go to her house this evening.'

And, glory be to God, wasn't it Jer Callanan himself that was in it—and the next minute didn't he clap some kind of cloth over my nose and mouth, and a strong fume out of it like turpentine, and he lifted me up in his arms and ran to the jennet's car with me, and after that, God bless us, I fell into some kind of trance; and when I got back my sense again I was lying in the car and Jer Callanan having one of his arms around me, and the jennet and he tearing along the road, like the very divil himself!

And mavrone!—you may say there was a terrible

fright on me for a bit after that, but I said a prayer to God in my heart, so I did, and I got back my courage on the spot, imbeersa, and if I did, I looked through the tail of my eye at the road, as well as I could make it out in the darkness. And 'twasn't long, thank God, till I spotted a light on the side of a hill over-right me out, and begannies, I knew where I was then for certain.

The light was in a farmhouse five miles from Bantry, where Curly Sweeney and his wife and children lived; and wasn't Curly one of my own sweethearts, before I got a man for myself, why, many long years before that. Sure, 'twas Curly Sweeney who composed an elegant song for me, and I a young girl and this was the way a few of the verses went, mossa:

> Oh, Kitty Kevane, sure I'll end my life,
> If you won't be persuaded to be my wife!
> For night and day and morning and eve
> 'Tis for you I sigh and for you I grieve.

> And when I'm asleep I'm dreaming of you—
> So, sleeping and waking, I'm always true!
> And sometimes I cry in the dead o' the night;
> Sweet Kitty I'll die if my love you'll slight!

> There's not a lily, there's not a rose,
> There's not a flower in the wide world grows,
> As sweet to look on as your sweet face—
> And your two grey eyes all my sorrows chase!

> The lilt of your voice is soft and clear;
> No skylark, when gleams of dawn appear,
> Was ever as sweet, as wild, as free,
> Singing to Heaven, as you to me!

So, begannies, I thought of a right plan now, so I did!

'I'll let on to be mortal sick entirely,' says I to myself, 'and I'll whisper to this scamp alongside of me (and he still thinking that 'tis Nano he has!) and I'll beg of him to bring me up to that farmhouse for a few minutes, till I get

a cupeen o' tay to make me well again for the journey—
wherever the mischief he's going!'And, faith, would you
believe it, didn't I carry out my plan with the melted
villain so I did!

I let on, (God forgive me!) that I was just going to fail
in some kind of fit, and, if I did, I put the heart across in
him with the screeches I let out of me, and I working like
as if I was in convulsions; and, 'Oh, for God's sake,' says
I, and I whispering—just like Nano herself would say it
—'take me up that boreen to the farmhouse under the
hill,' says I. 'Sure, even though they're black strangers
itself to each of us,' says I, 'the people living there won't
begrudge me a cupeen o' tay, to restore me!'

And, awonomsa, he said something to the boy and
away with us, on the mortal spot, and the boy and he
belted hell out of the jennet; and up the boreen with us,
in a mad gallop, and into the baan of Curly Sweeney's
farmhouse, why; and Jer Callanan took me in his arms,
and I kicking and lashing and groaning, the same as if I
was in the agonies of death, and he lepped out of the car
and away across the baan with him and up to the farmhouse door; and he lifted the latch of the door and
shoved aside the bolt of the half-door and in with him
into the kitchen, and he dropped me down on the settle
right alongside of Curly Sweeney himself, why!

And Curly was smoking his pipe for himself and his
wife and daughters and they minding a sow and fifteen
bonnives that were stretched on a borth of straw near
the hearth; and glory be to God, didn't Curly get such a
start, why, that the dhudeen lepped out of his mouth,
and 'twas smashed to smithereens on the flags!

And, 'I'm sorry for intruding on ye all in this way,
honest people!' says Jer Callanan, and he all sweetness
and politeness—the prime rascal!—'but this girl of
mine, the poor craythur, she's after getting some sort of
a weakness,' says he, 'and she begged of me to drive her

up here to this house,' says he, 'and I'll have to ask you to get a cup of tay for her,' says he, 'if 'tain't too much trouble, why?'

'And is she your wife, honest boy, or who is she?' says Mrs Sweeney, and she rising up from a stooleen near the sow, and she darting a queer, suspicious sort of look at myself. Sure, I could see her, plain enough, and I peeping out under the shawl, and I lying in the corner of the settle.

'Well, ma'am, I don't want to tell a lie to you, so I don't,' say Jer Callanan. 'She ain't my wife as yet,' says he; 'but, with the help o' God, she'll be my wife before the end of this coming week!'

And, begannies, and he saying that, didn't I start up from the settle, and while you'd be winking, mossa, didn't I pitch Nano Hegarty's shawl off of my head and shoulders and down on the floor at my feet.

And, 'You're after telling a lie—and an infernal lie this minute!' says I to Jer Callanan. 'For, if you went down on your two knees to me, I wouldn't marry you!'

Molaire, if you were to see the shock the blackguard got, when he saw who was really in it! And as big a start as Jer got, sure poor Curly Sweeney and his wife and daughter got one every bit as bad!

'Kitty, Kitty, woman! Is it yourself that's there all the time?' says Curly Sweeney, and he looking at me like as if he couldn't believe his two eyes, mossa.

And, sure, no more he couldn't the honest poor libe of a man. And after a minute, why, didn't my brave Jer Callanan get back his senses, and, 'This is all some cursed mistake, or some piece of prime blackguarding, so it is!' says he. 'I don't know anything at all about this woman—except,' says he, and his two black eyes and they blazing in his head with the dint of mad fury, and he saying it—'except that she's a daring, brazen-faced, impudent vagabone,' says he, 'and she's nothing else!'

Glory be to God, if you were to see Curly Sweeney, and Jer Callanan saying all that! Faith, I thought Curly would fly at Jer on the mortal spot; and so he would, faith, only I threw myself between 'em. And, if I did, why I up and told Curly Sweeney every single bit of my story, from start to finish, mossa—all about poor Nano Hegarty, and the warning she got in the dream, and the message she asked me to carry over to Mary Kate Lynch that evening and all that happened me on my ramble down the mountain road, and the plan I made up in my mind, after I getting back my senses in the jennet's car.

'And there's the ruffian that's the cause of all the trouble, Curly, my man,' says I, and I pointing straight at Jer Callanan. 'There he stands before you,' says I— 'the Widow Callanan's son, Jer, from Tubberbeg. And, begannies, if I was a man this minute and inside in your shoes, Curly Sweeney,' says I, 'I know what I'd do with that melted thief of a villain.'

And, molaire, the words were only just out of my mouth, why, when Curly Sweeney pulled down a horse-whip from the clevvy, and he made straight for Jer Callanan; but, faith, Jer lepped back a few steps and away with him out in the door and across the baan, like a flash of lightning. And, begannies, I ran to the door to look; and, if I did, I saw the boy that was holding the jennet and he making a dart at Jer and, imbeersa, he caught a grip of Jer by the collar of his coat, and Curly ran up at the same minute, and the two of 'em gave the divil's own trouncing to Jer Callanan, till he was screeching for mercy; and then Curly sent him out in the gate of the baan, with one kick, and landed him into a pond of mooluch water that was in the corner of the boreen just over-right the gate, why!

And that was the last I ever saw of Jer Callanan. I believe he left his home shortly after that and went away to America. And the boy—Flur Connor—that was driving the jennet's car, didn't he tell us he never knew, good nor bad, what was the real business Jer Callanan had on hands that night, when he hired himself and his car; 'and, sure, if I had to know what the blackguard was really up to,' says Flur Connor, 'there's no fear I'd have any hand in the job.

'Sure, didn't he let on to me,' says Flur, 'after he lifting yourself, ma'am, into the car, that you were his own sister, mossa, and that you were after breaking out of a hospital and that he was sent after you to carry you back again,' says Flur. 'So he hired me to drive him and his "sister" to a house near Drimoleague,' says Flur, 'where a cousin of his own,' he said, 'was living.'

This was Flur Connor's story, awonomsa; and 'twas never found out afterwards what Jer Callanan's full plans were, mossa, or what divilment he put before him to carry out, after he securing Nano Hegarty, as he intended that night.

And a few months after that, why, didn't Nano marry Dan Herlihy, after all; and molaire! you may see she wasn't sorry for it, nayther, so she wasn't, as the happy years went by.

So there's my story for ye, mossa; and tomorrow night I'm going to tell you the finest of all my poor mother's fireside stories and be sure ye'll all come early to hear it!

The False Sister

The story I'm going to tell ye tonight was one of my poor dear mother's fireside tales—God rest her soul!—and 'tis many a time long ago, and myself a little child, I heard her telling about *The False-Hearted Sister* or *The Cruel Princess* as she sometimes called it, and, young as I was at the time, mossa, 'tis many the tear I used to shed and I hearing all about poor Princess Mave and the terrible treatment she got—God help the craythur!—from her wicked, tyrannical sister.

Mavrone! but it is a queer story, so it is—one of the queerest I ever heard, in all my rambles—and my poor mother had a song about it, too, and it had over seventeen verses in it, imbeersa, and an air to it for all the world like she'd be keening over the dead, the Lord save us. Sure it used to put a kind of a cold shiver through and through me, to hear her at it long ago.

But here's my story for ye, why, and let ye listen to every word of it. I'm going to tell it to ye the very way my mother used to tell it to myself.

Well, once on a time, why, and a very good time it was, there was a great King and Queen in the south of Ireland and they having two daughters—the Princess Nuala and the Princess Mave—and one fine handsome son, Prince Connor.

And, mossa, Princess Nuala was a dark skinned, haughty, tyrannical young lady—God forgive her!—and 'twas the poor people around the King's palace that could tell ye all about her, so it was. Sure, by all accounts, she'd begrudge them the bite and the sup they'd get in the kitchen from the servants, and they, maybe, God help us, not to have a taste of food in their cabins only what they'd beg for themselves and their children.

'And if 'twas myself was the Queen in this palace,' the Princess Nuala used to say, 'not one mouthful would I gave these idle, lazy vagabonds and they're nothing else,' she used to say. 'I'd loose the bloodhounds and set them at them,' she used to say (the villain—and that was her name) 'and I'd get them tied up to one of the trees in the park and lashed with a cat-o'-nine tails,' she used to say: 'and that would soon learn them not to be beggars!'

But the youngest sister—the Princess Mave—was the loveliest young lady ye could see in a long day's journey, awonomsa fain. Long, silky hair she had, mossa, the very colour of yella gold, and it streaming down over her shoulders and below her knees, why; and she used to tie it with a blue silk ribbon, and a dove worked on the end of it in silken thread and the two eyes of the dove's head were two shining diamonds. And the Princess Mave's blue eyes were every bit as bright as the shining diamonds in the dove's head, and her skin was as white as the ceanavawn in the bog below the palace, and a red rose like as if 'twould be peeping at you out of each of her smooth cheeks. And she was as good, God bless her, as she was beautiful, the craythur, and there's no fear she'd ever refuse anyone in want, and, no signs on it, she had the love and blessings of the widow and the orphan, the hungry and the thirsty, those who went in rags and those who had no shelter from the cruel elements by night. To all such people, molaire, her heart, and her purse were ever open; and sure even if her purse was empty itself the loving smile and the soft word she'd give them was as good, every bit, as silver and gold and precious stones, why!

Mavrone! mavrone! But 'twas a mortal pity that anything bad should ever happen the craythur. But in this world, God help us all, 'tis often the wicked that thrive and flourish, for a while, anyway, and the good that are called on to carry the Cross. Well, why, here's my story for ye—and 'tis a sad story and a strange story, and 'tis worth your while, so it is, to listen with all your ears to old Kitty.

There was a fine, handsome young prince—the eldest son of another Irish king—and one day and they all hunting the deer in the royal forest didn't Prince Murrough (for that was the name was on him) chance to get a fall from his horse, and he was lying in the moss under the shade of a big oak tree, and he weak and bad enough, the poor young gentleman, when who should come the way, do ye think, but the Princess Nuala and the Princess Mave, and the two of them taking a ramble for themselves in the forest.

And, begannies, if they did, didn't both one and the other of them fall mad in love with Prince Murrough the instant minute they spotted him under the oak tree; and that same was no wonder at all, faith: for he was as noble-looking a young prince as ever was seen in that place. Six foot four inches he stood in his stockinged feet, I tell ye, and his hair was as black as the raven's wing and it all in curls as soft as silk about his fine manly head, and he had a heart of gold, so he had, awonomsa, and the goodness and kindness of it was shining out of his features why, the same as if a blessed lamp was inside of him and its light and beauty showing through the skin.

And, molaire, no sooner did he clap his two eyes on the lovely, pitying face of the Princess Mave when his heart lepped out to her, then and there, why; though of course, as the Princess Nuala was older than the Princess Mave, he was forced to be civil and respectful to her; and in one glance of his eyes, mossa, he saw the sort she really was, and he knew well enough she'd revenge her mind on her young sister, if he put any slight on herself by seeming to think more of the Princess Mave than of her. And, to make a long story short, why, the Princess Nuala invited Prince Murrough to come back to her father's palace with herself and her sister Mave; 'For,' says she, 'your own palace is over ten miles distant and the ride there would be too long for you,' says she, 'and you to be so weak at present.'

And the Princess Mave's two blue eyes just looked into Prince Murrough's face, but she said nothing; and if they did, imbeersa, Prince Murrough looked at Princess Mave and then he turned to his attendants and they helped him on his horse again, why, and he rode alongside of the two princesses, and they walking, every step of the way to their father's palace, where the King and Queen gave him a hearty welcome and he was lifted down off his horse and carried into one of the guest chambers on the spot.

And, faith, for a whole week, or more, Prince Murrough was not well enough to go back to his own palace; and ye may be very sure, so ye may, the Princess Nuala made the most of her chances when she had the young prince under the same roof as herself! But if she did itself, awonomsa, Prince Murrough contrived, some way or other to have a word in secret every day with the Princess Mave; though, faith, 'twas hard for him to manage it, so it was, seeing that the Princess Nuala was watching her sister the same as a cat watches a mouse. But, for all that, Prince Murrough did manage it, mossa.

Lovers is the divil, all out, why when their mind is bent on the one they love. The simplest of them can be as deep as the deep sea, begannies, when it comes to that; and the straightest of them, at all other times in life, can be as crooked as a ram's horn when they're planning out some scheme or other—the rogues of the world!—to bring their sweethearts to them, or to carry their selves to their sweethearts.

And so ye may be very sure, awonomsa, the Prince Murrough was in no way backward in the way of love and courtship while he was in the same palace with the two princesses; and, clever enough, mossa, he worked his way between the two of them, never letting on to the Princess Nuala one bit as to which of them both he loved the best; and when he was well again and when he went home to his own kingdom the only chance he had at all, at all, why, of keeping the peace between himself and the Princess Nuala was to send her presents of brooches and gloves and rings and jewelries of all kinds, imbeersa. And 'twould be hard to blame him, so it would, when you come to think of it; for if he didn't do the like of this, the divil a chance he'd have again of showing his face in the King's palace, if he wanted to pay a visit to the Princess Mave!

So, the Princess Nuala took his presents and, faith, she never suspected a bit, only to be as sure as could be that Prince Murrough was mad in love with herself, why; and usen't she to deck herself out with the brooches and the other things he was after sending her and she'd come over-right to her young sister, the Princess Mave, and dance and sing and show off Prince Murrough's love-gifts, and, "Tis a fine thing,' she used to say to her young sister, 'to be loved as I am loved by the handsomest, bravest young prince in Munster!'

And, faith, cute enough, the Princess Mave would never let on, a bit, why, only to praise the story with her sister and she knowing all the time, to be sure, that Prince Murrough was cract alive about herself. And 'twasn't long, mossa, till Prince Murrough paid a second visit to the King's palace; and after the Princess Nuala and himself having a long talk together in the state drawing-room didn't she go away to order up wine and sweetcake for her lover, to refresh him after his long journey; and, no sooner was the Princess Nuala out in one door, molaire, when the Princess Mave slipped in at the other, and straight to Prince Murrough with her, the poor child, and he opened out his two arms and she threw herself between them, and laid her golden little head on his breast.

And, mavrone, many's the sweet, loving word the two of them whispered to one another and she lying in his arms and he kissing her, and telling her he loved her beyond all others in God's wide world, and that he'd never, never consent to marry anyone alive, only herself. And he kissed her, again, so he did, and she kissed him, the craythur, and she promised to marry no other prince but himself if she had to wait till she was an old, old woman to get him.

And God help the two loving craythurs!—sure, they never felt the time passing, and they whispering their love to one another and covering one another's faces with kisses, just like two innocent children—and, mossa, they were nothing else, so they weren't—and, the Lord save us, didn't the Princess Nuala come back, unbeknownst to the drawing-room and she walking as soft and easy as a cat that would be stealing on the track of a bird, by the side of a hawthorn hedge in the summer time. And, alliloo! didn't she spot the two of them in each other's arms, and they kissing each other, and didn't she hear them vowing to marry each other and no one else in the world—and then, faith, all the fat was in the fire, at long last, why!

Divil a word she said, though, at the time; for she was a crafty, cunning, treacherous princess, with a heart as dark and as deep as the deep sea. And didn't she steal away from the drawing-room door, mind you, and after a minute or two didn't she come down the passage again, and she singing out loud the way they'd hear her and not suspect a bit, and in with her to the room to the two of them, and she all smiles and soft words—the melted villain!—and a servant in livery behind her and he carrying a golden tray in his hands and all sorts of wines and grand sweet-cakes and fruits on it, for Prince

Murrough's lunch.

And never in her life before, why, was the Princess Nuala as sweet and kind, moryeh, to her young sister as she was all the rest of that day; and after Prince Murrough riding away at last and promising to come back again the very next day, with God's help, to hunt the deer in the forest, himself and Prince Connor, the King's son, didn't the Princess Nuala take the Princess Mave by the hand, and, 'Come down along with me, sister dear,' says she, 'as far as the strand by the river,' says she, 'till we see if the royal barge is coming in.' And the Princess Mave went with her; though, mind you, she didn't half trust her, so she didn't, but she thought it better to be as civil as she could to her elder sister, so as to keep her on her hands, why. And the two princesses went down through the grand gardens of the palace and into the deer-park, where all the deer were feeding under the big oak trees, and the sun shining down on them through the branches, and the river winding below, and it full of fish. And they went by the miller's cottage and the mill-dam in the river, and the Princess Nuala laughing and talking all the time and her arm wound round the Princess Mave's little waist; and at last they came to a high bank over the deep water and the Princess Nuala led her young sister by the hand till she brought her to the very edge of the tide. And says she then—and she all smiles and sweet looks, God forgive the rascal!—'Look up the river, sister dear,' says she, 'and try if you could catch sight of the barge coming round the turn,' says she. 'Your eyes are better than mine.'

And the poor young Princess Mave—never dreaming of a bit, God help us!—turned her head to look up the river; and, if she did, faith, didn't the Princess Nuala, as quick as lightning, give her a shove with her elbow off of the stone she was standing on—and didn't she pitch her down into the deep rushing river below! Under the foaming water she went, mossa, but she rose again in a minute after and she cried out loud to her sister for help.

'Oh, sister—dear sister,' says she, 'reach me down your hand,' says she, 'and pull me out of the water. And if you do,' says she, 'the half of my land and fortune will be yours!'

But, mavrone! never a stir did the Princess Nuala give, only to look down at her younger sister and she drowning before her two eyes.

'No, no,' says she. 'I'll not reach you down my hand,' says she. 'And the whole of your land and fortune,' says she, 'will be mine!'

The drowning princess went under the water again, but if she did, why up she comes for a second time, and she cries out more pitiful than before to her sister.

'Oh, sister—dear, dear sister,' says she, and she in her last breath, the poor little craythur of the world, 'reach me down your glove,' says she, 'and my Prince Murrough will be your lover,' says she, 'and he'll give you all the love of his heart!'

And when the drowning princess put those words out of her a smile of pure poison came over the Princess Nuala's face and she looking, looking straight down into the mad river that was sweeping her young sister to her death.

And, 'No, no,' says she. 'I'll not reach you down my glove,' says she, 'and your Prince Murrough as you dare to call him,' says she, 'will be my lover all the surer when you're dead! So you may sink down to the bottom,' says she, 'for you'll get no hand or no glove of mine to help you. With my own ears and eyes today,' says she, 'I heard your love-words and I saw your kisses, you and Prince Murrough,' says she, 'and the two of ye in one another's arms,' says she. 'So now,' says she and her two eyes shooting flames of fire down on her dying sister, 'my vengeance is after falling on you and my heart's black curse along with it,' says she. 'And now you may sink,' says she, 'and when you're out of his way for ever I'll have some chance at last,' says she, 'of winning Prince Murrough back to me again.'

And, with that, didn't the hard-hearted, cruel villain turn away from the river, the Lord save us all; and the tide swept the drowning princess on before it, and by the time it carried her to the mill-dam the life was after leaving her—God bless the hearers!—and she was as dead as a stone. And by that time 'twas dark night, so it was, and no one saw her in the river, good nor bad, and her body wasn't found till late in the next evening, why.

(The Princess Nuala, I may as well tell ye, was after making up a lying story when she went home alone to the palace and she told the King and Queen and her brother Prince Connor, that 'twas the way her sister was after going to a nobleman's castle to the west of the royal park, to spend the night with her foster-sister, the nobleman's daughter.)

Well, why, just between day and dark on the next evening the miller's daughter went down to the river for a jug of water to scour the milk vessels in her dairy, and, faith, if she did, back she ran, hot foot a few minutes later and she as white as a sheet, mossa, and in with her to where her father was working in his mill.

And, 'Oh, father, father, father,' says she and she hardly able to speak, with the fright of it, 'there's a mermaid down in the mill-dam,' says she, 'and I'm in dread of her, she's lying so quiet and not a stir out of her,' says she, 'and her hair streaming all about her, and it floating on the water of the dam.' And down with the miller himself, faith, and he didn't give in at all to the story at first, imbeersa; but, begannies, when he came to the head of the dam he had to believe it. For there, sure enough, he saw a sight that put the heart across in him with the dint of terror.

And, 'Oh, the Lord save us all!' says she. 'What is it at all, at all?' says he, 'or is it alive or dead?'

And he up and called his two sons, awonomsa, and they drew off the water of the dam, so they did, and after they pulling in the body didn't they find out 'twas the dead Princess Mave instead of a mermaid; and they laid her down on the bank above the mill-dam and they roared and bawled and clapped their hands. God help us, and all the neighbours came running to see what was after happening, why; for as I'm after telling ye already everyone loved the Princess Mave and a good right they had to love her! Sure, the like of her in regard to charity and kindess and a big heart never came before or since.

And, God help us, why, they couldn't believe she was dead at all at first, so they couldn't and she lying there on the bank just as if she was fast asleep and dreaming with a smile on her lovely little face, the craythur, and her blue eyes closed, and her long yella curling hair streaming below her knees and it tied with the blue ribbon and the silver dove on it, and the two diamond eyes shining in the dove's head, like the eyes of a living thing. And when the people found the Princess Mave was really dead, all the women began to caoine and ullagone for her; and the wonder was, mossa, they didn't hear the crying and lamenting up at the palace. And, begannies, they surely would have heard it—for you'd hear it for miles and miles around—only that there was a great feast and amusements of all kinds going on, that same evening, at the royal palace, for the Princess Nuala knew well enough 'twas the only chance she had now to secure Prince Murrough for herself—for how could she tell what would happen when her sister's drowned body would be found in the river?

So she planned out a grand entertainment after the deer-hunt was over, and the royal court was all gathered in state, and the King and Queen and Prince Connor and Prince Murrough and they seated on velvet couches, and the Princess Nuala dressed in gold and precious stones, and she painted and powdered and scented, and jewels on her fingers and round her ankles and looped about her head, and she dancing on a big silver dish, with two attendants, dressed like fairies, and they fanning her with gauze fans, and a little boy with silver wings, like an angel to look at, and he blowing a gold trumpet and he marching up and down the palace chamber, why. And, faith, with all their fun and jollification they never heard the wild sorrowful ullagoning from the bank of the river, over the drowned Princess Mave.

Listen to me now, all of ye, why, and don't ye lose as much as one word of what I'm going to tell ye; for I'm coming now to the strangest part of my story, and every word of it is the truth.

While the poor dead Princess Mave was still lying there on the bank of the river, and all the women caoining over her, and all the men shedding tears, mossa, who should come that way but the famous harper Theigue Mac Caura, himself; and, sure, if he did, why, he stopped to see what was the cause of the big crowd of people and they all crying and lamenting. And after he pushing his way through the crowd his eyes fell on the dead princess and he could hardly see her face at first, with the veil of gold. And when he knew at last who was in it mavrone! he gave a terrible cry out of his heart and he threw up his two hands to heaven so he did, as if to call down the vengeance of God on whoever it was that was after being the cause of this.

And, 'Faire go deo! Faire go deo!' says he, and he choking with sobs. 'The like of her will never again be seen in this unhappy kingdom!'

And, with that, why, he fell to caoine her himself;

and, to this day there are old people who could sing for you some parts of the caoine that Theigue Mac Caura the harper composed that evening for the Princess Mave. My own poor mother—God rest her soul! —could say a lot of it, mossa, though I'm after forgetting the most of it, by this time.

He began by praising the Princess Mave for her beauty and her good deeds and the warm, loving heart she had for the very poorest people in her father's kingdom and then he went on to curse her murderer, if 'twas a thing that she was indeed after being done to death.

'And if such be the bitter truth,' says he, 'may the hand that slew her and the brain that thought of the deed suffer and burn in this life as well as in the next, and may the Almighty God, in his justice,' says he, 'lay bare to the whole Court and kingdom,' says he, 'the full truth as to this crime!'

And now the strangest part of my story is to be told; and, faith, 'tis hard to believe that such a thing could be done at all, at all, so it is; but, I suppose, Theigue Mac Caura was enchanted and he could do what no one else living at the time could do; and besides, his prayer to God was surely heard and granted.

It must have been so, mossa; because what did he now do, do you think? Ye never, never could guess; not if ye were to be thinking over it for forty years. Didn't he make a splendid harp out of the breast-bone of the drowned princess, and he strung her golden hair across it for strings, and, if he did, the Lord save us, when he ran his fingers over them the sound that was heard from them would melt a heart of flint. And, 'Let ye follow me all of ye to the palace,' says he then. 'I'll carry the harp to the King's Court,' says he, 'and I'll set it down among them all and play it for them.' And when he said this, why, he lifted up the harp and slung it across his shoulder, and a kind of fear and wonder fell over the crowd of people and not a single word, mossa, could they put to Theigue Mac Caura, and as true as I'm telling ye my story, didn't they all follow him, step by step, to the royal palace and when they got to it in they went after him—for Theigue was always sure of his welcome by the King and Queen—and he laid the harp on a white marble table just opposite the King and Queen and Prince Connor and Prince Murrough and the Princess Nuala; and, by the same token, wasn't she resting herself a bit at that minute, after her dancing, and her two dark eyes flaming in her head with love and joy and success—for she felt sure of Prince Murrough by this time, and she was after making up her mind, we may be very sure, to swear she had nothing to do with her sister, whenever the drowned body would be found.

And all the crowd gathered together at the back of the white marble table, mossa, and the King and Queen fixed their eyes on the strange-looking harp.

And, 'Tell me, Theigue, my man,' says the King. 'What sort of a harp is that at all, at all?' says he—'and what sort of tunes does it play?'

'You'll hear it now for yourself, your Majesty,' says Theigue Mac Caura.

And over with him to the side of the harp and he waved his two hands up and down over the strings and he said something or other, so he did, in a voice too low to be heard by anyone very plainly. 'And now let ye listen, all of ye,' says Theigue says he. 'The harp is going to play and sing for ye, without any help from me.'

And—praise be to the good God on high—didn't a sorrowful, moaning voice come out from the strings of the harp; and 'twas the voice of the Princess Mave herself. Sure, no one in that crowded Court could mistake it!

'My loved father, the King, is seated before me,' sang the sorrowful voice—the very same as if the Princess Mave herself—God bless us all!—was within the harp—

'and beside him is the Queen, my dear mother! And there yonder is my noble brother, Connor—and at his right side is my true lover, Prince Murrough, beloved of my heart, of all men, in death as well as in life!'

And all of a sudden (don't be frightened yerra, at what I'm going to tell ye now!) the voice rose to a wild screech of rage and grief and pain and fury, and everyone in the Court jumped and they trembling and gasping and the King and Queen had like to drop down dead with the dint of fright, the Lord save us!

And this is what the harp now said:

'And there—there—decked out in her gold and jewels, is my false-hearted sister Nuala, who murdered me last evening—who drowned me in the river, so as to get me out of her path the way she could win my own true lover, Prince Murrough, for herself after my death!'

And glory be to the good God on high, after these words were heard by the crowded Court there was a cry of grief and rage all round the place, and the King and Queen and Prince Connor and Prince Murrough turned in fury on the Princess Nuala, and the instant minute she looked into their faces, mossa, she knew all hope was over for ever for her, why; and she turned as white as death itself—only for her two eyes, and they were blazing like coals of fire in their sockets.

And right across the Court among the people she darted, like a mad thing, awonomsa, and she striving to make her escape. But she wasn't let go as easy as she thought! Not likely. When the crowd of people saw her running didn't they turn like lightning and out the door with them after her, and, if they did, mossa, she was captured just outside of the palace walls.

And, if she was, why, they built up in two minutes a pile of faggots and they set fire to them and into the blazing heart of them she was thrown just as quickly and surely as she was after throwing her sister into the river the day before; and they tossed fresh faggots on the fire, till the blaze shot up nearly to the top of the palace, and between the roars of the flames and the screeches of the people around the fire, a sound arose of the dying princess and the yells of that could be heard—and was heard, imbeersa, fain—for miles and miles away.

And the people were never punished by the King for what they did that day, so they weren't; and the harp was locked away in a state-room in the palace, all to itself, mossa, and 'twas kept there, they say for hundreds of years after, and what happened it in the end, why, I couldn't tell you. Sure, maybe, 'tis there always.

And Prince Murrough never took a wife—never—though he could have his pick and choice of all the Court ladies, imbeersa, if he wished, why. But, ye see he was true to his promise to the poor Princess Mave, never to wed anyone at all, at all if he couldn't wed herself. And into a monastery he went, faith, shortly after that and there he died many long years later, and was buried.

And this is the end of my story for ye; and now we have enough of sorrowful talk for one night, imbeersa; so we'll try and rouse ourselves with a song and a joke and a laugh.

The Stranger

Down by the wild sea coast of West Cork, between Castletownsend and Baltimore, there used to be—and I suppose 'tis in it still—a long, low thatched farmhouse, and it perched among the rocks and the crags right over the ocean; and, faith, 'tis often I thought, and I looking at the house, that it would be swept down into the sea, some winter's night, when the storm would be raging around its walls, like a pack of evil spirits.

Jer Bryan and his wife, and his two daughters, Ello and Annie, and his two sons, Jim and Richie, lived in the farmhouse. A hardworking, steady, thrifty family they were, mossa; and Ello Bryan was as fine-looking a young girl as you could see in all West Cork; and, faith, if she was, she wasn't without a sweetheart, imbeersa.

Paul Kearney was the name of Ello Bryan's lover, and as fine a girl as Ello was, Paul was just as fine for a boy. They were an elegant couple all out, so they were; and the first time myself spotted the two of 'em, and they taking a ramble together, one Sunday evening along the cliffs by South Reen, I thought I never before in my life laid eyes on such a handsome pair.

And as purty as Ello Bryan was, to look at, she was just as nice and as good and kind, mossa, in her acts; and, if you were to see her and she nursing and petting her poor little bedridden sister, Annie (sure, the cray-thur was dying of decline, at this time, God help us!) you couldn't keep the tears out of your eyes, so you couldn't, unless you were made of stone.

But, here's my story for you, and 'tis worth your while, so it is, to listen to every word I'm going to tell you now.

One November evening, Paul Kearney came over to the Bryans' farmhouse, intending to ask Ello to marry him in the following month; but, when he arrived at the house, mossa, he found that poor Annie Bryan was after getting a bad turn that very evening; and the Bryans' landlord's daughter, Miss Mary Travers, from Kildarra, and a Miss Beamish, a paid companion of hers, were inside in Annie's bedroom for those two ladies used often come to visit the poor dying girl, ever since Captain John Travers came to live at Kildarra House, about a year before this November evening, mossa.

Before that time, Captain Travers lived in England

and other places, but 'twas said that, after his only son, Master Alan Travers, meeting a violent death, away in some foreign country, the Captain was too heartbroken to live any longer among his gay, stylish friends; so himself and his daughter, Miss Mary, and Miss Mary's companion, Miss Beamish, arrived in Kildarra House, and you may say their tenants around the district were proud and glad of this, imbeersa, for if ever there was an angel of mercy and goodness on this earth, Miss Mary Travers was one, God bless her, and her companion was just as kind and as good, every bit. But, sure, whatever they'd do, God help us, they couldn't make poor Annie Bryan strong and well again, and do their best, why; though, right enough, the poor little girl got a bit stronger after that November night.

So, Paul Kearney didn't like to bring up his own bit of business, as to fixing the day for his marriage, when he saw Ello Bryan in such trouble of mind that night about her poor sister.

'I'll wait till tomorrow night, so I will,' says Paul to himself, 'and maybe Ello would be in better humour then about Annie.'

And a terrible storm arose that same night, mossa. For years and years, there wasn't the like of it along that part of the coast; and all the next day it blew and blew, without stopping, and about seven o'clock in the evening, at last the furious gale died down a bit, and queer, moaning, crying sounds, like the banshee lamenting for someone's death, passed around the Bryans' farmhouse, as Ello sat all by herself in the kitchen, and she baking a bastable of bread for the supper and for the next day. Mrs Bryan was up on the loft with Annie and Jer Bryan and his two sons were after going down the rocks to the little cove, about an hour or two before; and, all of a sudden, as Ello sat by the fire, she heard the sound of loud, excited men's voices outside, and heavy footsteps came to the door, and the next minute, awonomsa, the door was shoved open, and in came Paul Kearney and Jer and they carrying the body of a fine young man between them, and he as still and as white as a corpse.

Down on the settle they stretched the body, and then Paul Kearney told Ello that 'twas himself was after seeing the young man and he floating in on the waves, with a cork belt fastened around him, and 'twas as much as ever he could do, Paul said, to pull the body to the shore.

'And, whether he's dead or alive, I don't know, imbeersa,' says Paul Kearney. 'Sure, only for your father, Ello, I'd never manage to get him up here at all, I'm in dread!'

And Ello's two brothers came in at the same minute and they all set to and they did whatever they could think of to coax the poor young man back to life again; and, begannies, they didn't fail in their task, so they didn't, and in half an hour's time, why, the young man was lying on a straw palliasse before the fire and the colour coming back to his cheeks again and the life to his two eyes, and 'twasn't long, faith, till he lifted himself up on his elbow and he looked around him from one face to another.

And, 'Where am I at all?' says he. 'What is your name and the name of this place, good people?'

And, faith, Paul Kearney up and he told him, and the strange young man listened to Paul, and then he asked no more for a minute or two, imbeersa, as if he was thinking over Paul's words. And all this time, as you may guess for yourselves, why, Ello Bryan's two blue eyes were fixed on the stranger's face, and she was thinking to herself that, whoever he was or wherever he came from, he was the handsomest young man she ever saw in all her life before, and that no softer, sweeter voice ever before fell from a young man's lips than his voice was, mossa, even in the few words he was just after speaking.

But the stranger told them nothing at all about himself—not a word, imbeersa—only that he was shipwrecked on his way to Liverpool, from abroad. What his name was, or who he was, or anything at all about himself, awonomsa, he never as much as hinted at, to any of 'em.

'If I could stay here for a few weeks until I'd be strong again, I'd be very thankful,' says he to Ello that night. 'And, of course, your people will be repaid for their kindness,' says he. 'But I don't want anyone at all to know I'm here,' says he. 'So, I'll ask you to keep it a secret and to caution your family to say nothing about it outside the house,' says he. And, Ello Bryan promised him faithfully, mossa, that his wishes would be carried out in all ways, and then the young man's mind seemed to be easier; and, day by day, he got stronger and stronger again, and Ello nursing him the same as if she was his mother, why!

An elegant, handsome young man he was, too, and anyone should be fond of him, so they should, and he was like a child, he was so gentle and quiet; and the Bryans were after fixing up a little bed for him on the gable loft, so he was out of the way of people coming into the house, and the neighbours around never knew he was there at all, so they didn't, and when Miss Mary Travers and Miss Beamish used to call to the house to see poor Annie, they never guessed there was another sick person under the same roof as well as Ello's sister.

And soon, faith, the strange young man got so much better, why, that he was able to sit up for a few hours every day, and sometimes, Ello read bits out of the papers or out of storybooks for him, and, sometimes, she'd sing a song or two to cheer him up; and a good warrant she was, too, to sing a song. 'Twould delight you to hear her, imbeersa. And, begannies, during these weeks, Ello was so taken up with the strange young man in the gable loft that she had very little time left for her sweetheart, Paul Kearney, and Paul had no chance at all of putting the question to Ello about fixing up their marriage; and, faith, 'twasn't long till Paul began to notice things, and, after that he took to watch Ello, night by night, and, whatever he found out in her looks and her manner, the end of it was that he got mad jealous of the strange young man, and the terrible thought came into Paul Kearney's mind, God help us, that Ello Bryan was after falling in love with the handsome stranger and that she was false to her old lover, mossa, and that he'd never win her now for his wife. And, from that time out, mind you, didn't Paul Kearney keep away from Ello's home; and, though the girl, to be sure, noticed Paul's coolness towards herself, yet, she seemed to be like one in some sort of a dream, or a trance; and, whatever spell this strange young man was after throwing over her, Ello didn't seem to trouble her head much whether Paul came to see or or whether he didn't, mossa. All she thought about at this time, was the young man poor Paul was after saving from the sea.

'Wisha, what did we do to Paul that he's shunning us like this, I wonder?' says Ello's mother, one day, shortly before Christmas. 'I never remember him to stay away from the house for so long before,' says she. 'Tell me the truth, Ello,' says she, 'is it the way yourself and Paul had any sort of a falling-out, or what?'

'Indeed, no, mother, we never had a word between us,' says Ello. 'I'm just as wise as you are,' says she, 'over the business. So, faith, as I'm not to blame in any way,' says Ello, and she giving her head a toss and she saying it, 'Paul may see out his humour to the end, so he may! There's no fear,' says Ello, 'I'm going to fall down on my two knees and beg of him, for God's sake, to come to see us!'

But, Ello's mother was no fool, so she wasn't, and, faith, it flashed on her at last that, maybe Paul Kearney was vexed with Ello on account of spending so much of her time with the strange young man; and, after Mass on the next Sunday—'twas the very Sunday before Christmas, so it was—didn't Mrs Bryan follow Paul Kearney down the road from the chapel, and, when she got him in a lonesome spot, all to herself, she stood over-right him out and and she asked him plain and straight why he was such a stranger during the weeks before, and was it the way himself and Ello were after quarrelling. And, faith, Paul Kearney was too honest-hearted a chap to hide the truth from Mag Bryan, and he up and told her that, so far as he could see himself, Ello had no great welcome for him to the house ever since the night he carried up the strange young man from the seashore.

'And, faith, 'tis often I heard,' says Paul Kearney to Mag Bryan, 'that if you save a man from drowning he'll live to do you an ill turn, so he will,' says Paul.

'But, sure, he's a stranger to us, Paul,' says Mag Bryan. 'What do we know about him, good nor bad. I'll promise you one thing, whatever, Paul,' says Mag. 'If you'll drop over to us tonight, you'll see that matters will be all right again, so they will.'

'Well, maybe, I would, ma'am,' says Paul Kearney, 'I'll be thinking over it.'

And, away with Mag Bryan, and, as soon as she reached her home, she called Ello alongside and she told her what Paul was after saying to her and he coming from Mass.

'And, 'tis a shame for you, so it is, to be carrying on the way you are, Ello!' says her mother to her. 'And I'm after promising Paul that this will end it now, and he'll be over tonight again, I expect; so, be sure you'll be nice and civil to him!' says Mag. But, Ello was fit to be tied, at the same minute, why, she was so put out at what her mother was after telling her.

And, when, sure enough, Paul Kearney did come sgoriachting to the house that night, Ello was freezing in her manner to him, and, before ten o'clock, Paul Kearney said goodnight to them and went away home.

And, though Ello's mother spent a full hour scolding her and abusing her, after Paul was gone, 'twas all no use, imbeersa. Ello wouldn't give in as much as one inch, so she wouldn't, and Mag Bryan had to hold her tongue in the end, why!

And, as the days went by, between that and Christmas, things grew from bad to worse, and, on Christmas Day itself, of all days in the year, Ello and her mother had hot words together just and they getting ready to go to Mass.

'Well, this puts an end to it now, at last, Ello,' says Mrs Bryan. 'Ever since that strange young man came into the house, there's some kind of misfortune after falling on us all, and there's nothing only crossness and suspicion and fighting and squabbling and every sort of divilment, awonomsa. So, faith, this can't go on any longer, and, if he's well enough for the road tomorrow, he'll have to clear out, bag and baggage. And, if you don't tell him so, today or tonight, I'll tell him myself, so I will, and in plain words, too, I promise you!'

And, faith, Ello was so angry and upset at what her mother said that she was inclined to fight with everyone that day; and Paul Kearney and herself met, face to face, and they coming out after Mass, but Ello couldn't bring herself to say as much as one civil word to him, and she swept past him, the same as if he had the fever, the Lord save us, and she was in dread she'd catch it from him, or something like that. And, all through the day, Ello was in a temper, begannies, and, late in the evening, just and the moon rising, didn't she slip down from the gable loft, where she was sitting by the strange young man's bedside (for he was going to dress himself and join the family downstairs by the fire, in honour of Christmas night), and, out of the house, all by herself, went Ello, and down the rocky path to the seashore, and she never stopped till she reached the very edge of the sea.

The moon was shining down on the wide ocean, and it looking for all the world like a big, silver lamp hanging in the sky; and the waves came rolling in and their wide crests hissing and tossing, like the manes of mad war-horses and, faith, one great tall wave came rearing in so far that Ello had only time to climb up over a rock to save herself from a shower-bath, and when she lepped down at the other side of the rock she found herself at the mouth of a little cave that runs in for a few yards under the rock just in that spot.

And, now I'm coming to the strangest part of my story, and 'tis worth your while to listen to me, so it is!

The Lord save us, just and Ello landing on the beach at this spot didn't she see the inside of the little cave, and it as bright as day in the moonlight; and just inside the mouth of the cave, as true as I'm telling you my story, imbeersa, didn't Ello spot Paul Kearney himself, and his face as white as a dead man's and he standing with one shoulder leaning against the rock and—God bless the hearers!—he had a pistol in his right hand and 'twas pointed at that very minute straight and sure for his temples, and his little finger was just going to press the trigger—to take his own life, the Lord be good to us all. And, with one spring, didn't Ello come alongside of him; and, if she did, faith, didn't she sweep the pistol out of his hand with one blow of her fist, why, and she sent it flying out on the beach among the pebbles at the edge of the sea.

And, at that minute, imbeersa, didn't the whole truth of the matter flash on Ello's mind—and all Paul's jealousy and despair was as clear as the noonday to her —and all her heart's love for Paul was plain enough now to Ello, and she said to herself that she well deserved to lose Paul Kearney and his love for ever and ever, and she after allowing herself to treat the poor, true-hearted boy so cruelly, and all for the sake of some mad, foolish fancy that came over her, for a bit, for that strange young man up at the house.

And, 'For God's sake, what are you doing here, Paul?' says Ello, and she bursting out crying and her arms flung around his neck. 'Surely, surely,' says she, and a shiver going through her from head to foot, "twasn't the way you were going to take your own life just now!'

'And that's the very thing I was going to do, Ello,' says Paul Kearney. 'I said to myself 'twould be better for me to be dead, mossa fein, than to be scorned and slighted by you, girl, day after day, and a strange man,' says he, 'that none of us know anything about, taking up all your time and drawing away all your love and all your loyalty from myself!'

So, then and there, awonomsa, Ello told Paul, straight out from her heart, that he was the only boy in the wide world she ever cared about, and she told him she'd never, never again give him cause to misdoubt her, and then, when he put the question to her, began-nies, she promised to marry him as soon as ever her people could fix up the business after Christmas.

So, for an hour or more, the pair of 'em chatted and made love to one another in the cave, and the moon shining down on their happy faces, mossa, like as if it was giving them its blessing and wishing them well in their future married life together. And, after this, why, they went up the rocky path to Ello's home, and when they stepped into the kitchen, and they smiling at one another, like two happy children, the craythurs, didn't they spot the strange young man and he sitting alongside of the big turf fire, and Mag Bryan at one side of him and Jer at the other, and Jim and Richie over-right him out, and they all listening, with their mouths wide open, to whatever he was telling them.

And up jumped Mag Bryan when Ello and Paul came in, and, faith, in one half of a glance, she guessed all was settled up between 'em.

And, 'Ello, Ello,' says Mag, in a whisper, 'who do you think our lodger really and truly is?' says she. 'Sure, he's just after telling us his secret. Ain't he Master Alan Travers himself—Captain Travers' own son that he thought was killed out in Africa last year,' says Mag. 'But, 'twas a false report, so it was, thank God,' says she, 'though Master Alan didn't deny it at the time. Another trouble was on him,' says she, 'and he couldn't very well write home at all without telling his people all about it, and this he didn't want to do, imbeersa; so he thought it safer not to write a line at all.'

And, just and she whispering all this to Ello, didn't footsteps come to the door outside, and the door was opened, why, and, in stepped Miss Mary Travers and her companion, and they having a Christmas present each for poor little Annie Bryan. And, glory be to God, when Miss Mary Travers spotted her own brother, Master Alan, that she thought was dead and buried a year or more before that, didn't she let out a screech of joy out of her and she ran over to him and threw herself into his arms.

But, that wasn't all, awonomsa! A stranger thing was to follow.

The instant minute Master Alan Travers laid eyes on Miss Beamish's sweet, true face didn't he nearly drop with the dint of shock he got!—and, no wonder, he would, faith. For, wasn't 'Miss Beamish' only a fancy name she took for a bit, for her own reasons, and wasn't she, in reality, Master Alan's own wedded wife that he was after marrying abroad two years before that, mossa!

Some lying, venomous-hearted mischief-maker was after bringing about a bitter quarrel between Master Alan and his wife, and his wife left him in anger and went back to her own people, and Master Alan started off, in a mad rage, to Africa and he not caring what was to happen him, good nor bad, why! And then, after his escape from death—though the news of his death was printed in the papers—he couldn't bring himself to write to his own people, imbeersa, as he didn't want to tell them the bad news about his wife; particularly as they were never after meeting her, at this time, and he was after giving her the highest praise in his letters. So he didn't write home at all; but, after a year or so, he made up his mind at last to go back to his father and his sister, and he was on his way to England when he was ship-wrecked.

So all was cleared up now, mossa, and Master Alan's wife told him she made the plan to get a situation as Miss Mary's companion, so that she'd have a good chance of hearing the truth about him—as she never believed the story of his death—and also because her love for him, in spite of their quarrel, made her long to be with his people, imbeersa, for she couldn't but look upon them as her own as well. .

So, the end of it was, why, that Master Alan and his wife were happier than ever again, and there was great rejoicing up at Kildarra House for months and months after that.

And Ello and Paul Kearney were married early in Shrove and poor Annie got a bit better, thank God; so there was nothing, you see, to throw a shadow over all their happiness, the craythurs, and they well deserved their good luck, so they did, after all the trouble and botheration that went before it!

And there's my story for ye and I wish ye all a Merry Christmas and a Happy New Year!

The Bog House

The Bog House, as 'twas always called in that part of the Co. Cork, is an old ivy-covered barrack of a house—hundreds of years old, they say, and it standing in the heart of a grove of hawthorns and elders and hazel-bushes, just by the very edge of the lonesome bog of Purth-na-Shee. Molaire! 'tis often, and I on my travels, that I gave a night in the Bog House, and, to tell nothing but the truth of the people that used to live there long ago—the Briens—they were a fine, dacint, grauver family, everyone one of them, God rest their souls; for nearly all of 'em are dead and buried now, only some of the far-out cousins of the family.

People used to say that the Bog House was haunted, God bless the hearers, and, begannies, if you were to see it in the twilight, as myself often saw it, with the ancient trees and bushes and their branches all growing a-one side, with the dint of the gales sweeping across the bog from the north-west, and the black old dungeon of a house, and it buried in ivy, and the high, steep roof and the chimney's rising, like some enchanted castle, above the trees, and the dreary bog stretching away, away below the house, and the curlews and the snipe and the wild ducks and the pilibeen-meeachs and they crying and screeching through the wild caoining and ullagoning of the wind—if you were to hear and see all that, I tell you, you'd soon run for your lives, so you would, to some place where your hair wouldn't be standing on end with terror and where you wouldn't be in dread to look over your shoulder, lest you'd set your two eyes on a spirit, God between us and harm this night!

But here's my story for you, and 'tis a queer, ghostly story I'm going to tell you: so let ye all gather close to me, and stir up the turf into a blaze, the way you'll have some sort of courage, mossa, to listen to my tale.

At the time the strange thing happened that I'm just going to tell you about, Eamonn O'Brien and his wife and their son and daughter, Jack and Julia, lived in the Bog House. In old times, to be sure, the Bog House used to be a gentleman's residence, but the old stock that owned it fell into debt, mossa, and the property was bought by a great-grandfather of Eamonn Brien's and from father to son it came down to Eamonn himself at last.

Julia Brien was a fine, tall, handsome girl, so she was, with something noble and queenly in her walk and in her look, and she was beloved by all the poor people around the place and by all the travelling men and travelling women that called to the Bog House, for food, or clothing, or shelter. But with all her goodness and all her youth and beauty, begannies, Julia didn't seem to care about any of the young men in the district, and 'twasn't one morsel of good for them to be coming sgoriachting to the Bog House, or striving to have a biteen of court-ship with Julia when they'd meet with her at balls and parties and sprees, or in the market-town of a Saturday, or outside the chapel gates of a Sunday after Mass.

'Faith, 'tis my opinion, Kitty,' says Julia's mother to myself, one evening that I rambled into the Bog House, about this time, mossa—''tis my opinion,' says she, 'that our Julia will be a nun, like her father's sister Julia before her—and she's now Sister Mary Loyola in the Good Shepherd's Covent in Cork.'

'Wisha, maybe she would take a notion that way,

ma'am,' says I, and the two of us and we warming our toes by the turf fire in the big kitchen. 'May God direct the craythur!' says I. 'Sure, if 'tis a thing that she gets the holy call to the convent she'll have to go, I suppose, whether you like it or whether you don't, ma'am, God help us!'

'Well, whatever she may do in that way, Kitty,' says Julia's mother, and she wiping away a tear from her eye and she saying it, 'nayther her father nor myself will go again her, so we won't. Right enough, Kitty,' says she, "twould almost break my heart, if Julia went in to the nuns—God forgive me, for saying it!—but still, for all, I wouldn't fly in the face of providence,' says she, 'by interfering with her, mossa, in any way in the world, why!'

Well, this was all very fine, imbeersa, but the next time I rambled to the Bog House—about eight or nine months after that—I heard a different story.

About a mile to the west of the Bog House the farm-house of Liscree stands in a pleasant, sheltered hollow, and for ten years no tenant lived at Liscree, mossa, on account of some row that ruz between Mr Stokes, the landlord, and a tenant of the name of Cadogan that rent-ed Liscree for thirty years, or over it. So Mick Cadogan and his family were evicted, and for ten long years after that, as I'm just after telling you, Mr Stokes could get no one into Liscree in their place.

But at last a young man, of the name of Martin Magrath, from the County Tipperary, took the Liscree farm, and himself and his cousin Luke—both fine, tall, hearty young men—came to live at Liscree, and a sister of Luke's, Bride Magrath, came to housekeep for the two young men at the farm. And, molaire, the instant minute Martin Magrath set his two grey eyes on Julia O'Brien's face he fell mad in love with her, and Julia seemed to take a liking to him on the mortal spot.

''Tis only a bare month, Kitty, since the Magraths came to the place,' says Julia's mother to me, and she telling me her story, the night I rambled back to the Bog House; 'and yet, somehow,' says she, 'they seem to be old friends of ours already. Martin Magrath is as fine a young man as ever I laid my eyes on, Kitty,' says she, 'and his cousin Luke is a good-looking, hearty young man also. Bride Magrath—Luke's sister—is the plainest of the three of 'em,' says Mrs Brien; 'and I'm not so sure of Bride as I am of the others. If I don't make a big mistake, Kitty,' says she, 'Bride Magrath thinks the world and all of her cousin Martin, though any fool may see,' says she, 'that Martin Magrath looks on Bride the same as if she was his sister, and nothing more than that, imbeersa fain!'

And, faith, when I heard all this, mossa, I was wishing in my heart to see the Magraths, so I was, and on the very next night, why, didn't the three of 'em land over to the Bog House about nine o'clock. Martin Magrath was an elegant, tall, broad-shouldered young man, and he having a head of black curls, and two bright black eyes and they dancing with good humour, and Luke was like his cousin, only to be bigger, and coarser and rougher, in his ways; but as for Bride Magrath, the minute I took one look at her something warned me that she was no great shakes.

Her eyes seemed to be always shifting hither and over in her head, and they were a greenish-yellow colour, just like the eyes of a cat. She had thin, sharp features and a peevish, twisted sort of a mouth; and whenever she looked at Julia Brien a kind of frown passed over Bride's face; and, begannies, before half an hour was over a suspicion crossed my mind, and I got surer and surer of it every second I may say, after that.

'Bride hates Julia like poison,' says I to myself. 'She's jealous of Julia, because Bride is mad in love herself with Martin Magrath. Luke Magrath is after falling in love with Julia,' says I to myself, 'just the same as Martin—though 'tis no use for him, God help us, and the sooner he gets back his senses again the better for himself, imbeersa. As for Julia,' says I to myself, ''tis easy enough to see she's after taking a fancy to Martin Magrath, and I'm sorry for it in a way, so I am; because if I was in Julia's shoes,' says I to myself, 'I wouldn't like to make an enemy of Bride Magrath—no, nor of her brother Luke, nayther—if I could help it!'

But I kept my thoughts to myself, so I did though, faith, my eyes were wide open all the time; and as the days and the weeks went by 'twas plain enough to be seen that Martin Magrath and Julia Brien were sweethearts, though, at the same time, Julia didn't seem to love Martin as he loved her. I suppose 'twas the way that she had the longing all the time, down deep in her heart to go into the convent, like her aunt before her and though she was fond of Martin Magrath 'twas more the love of a sister than a sweetheart.

Well, why, Julia and Martin were everywhere together, as the months passed on; and when the long summer evenings came round you'd see the pair of 'em and they rambling across the paths through the lonesome bog of Purth-na-Shee; and 'tis often I spotted 'em and they resting on the big Grey Stone—the Clough Lia, as we used to call it—right in the heart of the bog. The Clough Lia was said to be a 'cast' flung by Fuen Macool, the Irish giant, hundreds of years before that, from the top of a rocky hill to the north of the bog. 'Twas—and it is still, imbeersa—a big rough stone, and it standing all by itself in the lonesome part of the bog, and a little grove of alders just below it, and the wild bog stretching all round it, like the ocean, with every wind from the heavens sighing and singing and piping through the rushes and the furze and the bushes, all day long.

And when I'd spot Martin and Julia and they seated, side by side, on the Clough Lia, as true as I'm telling you my story, a kind of a lonesome feeling used to come over me, and a voice seemed to say right into my very ear, the Lord between us and harm: *'They'll never be happy together in this world!'*

And you'll soon find out, so you will, whether this was true or not.

Martin Magrath was about a year at Liscree when he opened his heart to Julia Brien and asked her to be his wife in the following month. 'Twas a Sunday evening, in the late harvest-time and the two of 'em were crossing the bog together from Julia's home where Martin was after spending most of the day, since Mass time, with Julia's people. And just and they after coming to the little grove of elders below the Clough Lia Martin threw his two arms round Julia and he told her of his love for her at long last. So Julia confessed to him that she was fond of him why, and that she'd be thinking over the matter and she promised to give him her answer on the very next evening, if he'd stroll over to the Bog House about nightfall.

'And now I'll be going back home for myself,' says Julia, and she pulling herself out of his arms, and she saying it. ''Tis getting late and 'twill soon be dark,' says she, 'so goodbye for the present, and good luck!' says she and she waving her hand to Martin and he going.

And, what do you think, wasn't Bride Magrath hiding in the little grove all the time and she listening to every word—the melted villain, and that was her name!—and the instant minute Martin was after going out of sight, why, didn't Bride follow Julia, and she overtook her just and Julia passing the Clough Lia; and 'Don't be in such a hurry home, Julia Brien!' says Bride, 'I have a couple of words to say to you!'

And poor Julia let a cry out of her and she turning

round in her surprise, mossa; and there stood Bride Magrath and she panting with fury and her two mad cat's eyes and they blazing in her head like balls of fire, the Lord save us.

And, 'I heard every word Martin Magrath is just after saying to you, Julia Brien,' says Bride Magrath. 'I was crossing the bog, on my way to your own home,' says she, 'and I hid myself in the alders when I saw the two of you coming along towards me. I was going to your father and mother to the Bog House,' says she, 'to tell them my story; and now,' says she, 'I'll tell it to yourself first!'

And Julia had like to drop down dead with fright, so she had, awonomsa, for Bride Magrath looked more like a mad-woman than a girl in her proper senses.

'And here's the truth for you at last, Julia Brien,' says Bride, and she hardly able to speak the words, with the mad rage that was on her. 'Martin Magrath is a two-faced, deceitful, false, lying, treacherous villain,' says she, 'and he's pledged to marry me for the past two years,' says she, 'and now I'm just after listening to him and he asking you to be his wife next month!'

And Julia let another cry out of her, and she listening to this and not a word could she speak in answer.

'Martin put me off from day to day, from week to week, from month to month,' says Bride Magrath. 'Do you think it likely I'd ever come here to Liscree to housekeep for him, only for his promise to marry me as soon as the house was furnished and in order?' says she. 'And if you don't believe what I'm after telling you,' says Bride, 'maybe you'd believe your own eyesight,' says she, and she whipping a letter out of her pocket and she holding a sheet of paper, and it half covered with handwriting, before Julia's eyes, and she saying it. And, right enough, 'twas a love-letter from Martin Magrath to Bride, and his name at the end of it, mossa, and the last few lines of the letter ran like this: 'I love no one in the wide world only yourself, Bride, and I think it too long till you'll be my own wedded wife, dearest. And I remain, ever and always your own loving, Martin Magrath.'

And Julia's sight had like to spread in her head, and she reading this and a kind of weakness came over her and she fell back against the Clough Lia, and she staring, without a word out of her lips, into Bride Magrath's furious face.

'So now you know the truth, and you can please yourself as to marrying Martin Magrath, or not,' says Bride; 'but if you *do* marry him,' says she, 'may the curse of heaven fall on you and yours,' says she, 'and may every day and every hour and every minute of your married life be full of trouble and sorrow and loss and sickness and every misfortune,' says she. 'And that's my last word to you, Julia Brien!' says she, and she turning away from Julia and leaving her all alone, and she more dead than alive, God help us, and she leaning against the Clough Lia, and the strength after leaving her limbs, why!

But, faith, Julia Brien was a spirited girl, and the blood in her veins couldn't put up with too much bad usage, mossa; and after a bit she plucked up her courage, so she did, and 'There's no fear,' says she to herself, 'that I'm going to take another girl's leavings, so I'm not!' says she. 'And when Martin Magrath comes for his answer tomorrow night, he'll get it!' says she, 'no mistake about that.'

And home with her on the mortal spot to the Bog House, and she never let on a bit to her father and mother or her brother Jack.

And, sure enough, Martin Magrath came over to the Bog House the next night, just after nightfall, and, if he did, Eamonn and Jack Brien were out of home at a mehul and Julia's mother and the servant-girl were in the dairy about some work of their own; so Julia was all by herself in the house when Martin came into the kitchen.

And, mavrone, you may say 'twas a sore and sorry meeting between 'em both!

Julia didn't say very much, mossa—she wasn't the sort of a girl who would scold a man like a fisherwoman or the like of that, why!—but what she did say went through and through Martin Magrath like the point of a sword, so it did.

And, 'I'm after finding out all about you,' says she, 'and I have proof positive of your treachery to another girl and your promise to marry her long before you met me,' says she. 'So now you can go back to her and be fair and honest to her at long last,' says she. 'And I'll have nothing more to say to you, Martin Magrath,' says she. 'Only I'm thankful to God that I found out in good time,' says she, 'what you really and truly are, at heart!'

And Martin tried to put the lie on what she was accusing him of, but, molaire, she wouldn't listen to him and she refused to give him any more information on the matter, good nor bad; and in the end, why, Martin Magrath's own spirit was roused up, and 'You'll be sorry for this yet, Julia Brien,' says he, 'and you'll find out that you're after wronging me, when, maybe, 'twill be too late to win my forgiveness!'

And out the door with him, and he saying this—and 'tis often afterwards his parting words rang in Julia's two ears again—and when Mrs Brien and the servant-girl came in from the dairy Julia never said one word about what was after happening in the kitchen while they were out.

And on the very next evening, as true as I'm telling you my story, didn't Luke Magrath come over to the Bog House—and what was his news, do you think?

His news was this, awonomsa fain; his sister Bride was

Liscree every day, as usual, to attend to his farm.

And, faith, he took 'em at their word, so he did and he came to sleep at the Big House every night, and the first time myself laid eyes on him, after that, I thought I never, in all my born days, saw a man so altered in his looks and manner as Luke Magrath!

The very bones in his face and in his hands seemed to be standing out from the skin, and there were black marks under his eyes, and he'd never look you straight in the face now, like he used before, and he was always starting and turning his head, like one that would be listening for something, or in dread of seeing something, God between us and all harm this night!

And, to make a long story short, why, Julia took pity on Luke, and she was kind and gentle to him always and 'twasn't long, imbeersa, till 'twas plain enough to be seen that he was mad in love with Julia—and, sure, the truth of it was, that from the very first day he laid eyes on her, Luke Magrath loved the girl, no mistake at all, at all, about that!

And, begannies, some of the neighbours were still whispering to one another that Martin Magrath was after deserting Julia and that she was pining away, after him; and, I suppose, this thought was such gall to Julia's spirit that, bejakers, she made up her mind in the end that 'twould be as good for her to marry Luke and to let them all see she wasn't dying around Martin and that she could get just as good a husband as ever Martin would be.

So, what do you think, didn't the news reach my ears, one day, on the road from Skibbereen, and I rambling back to the Bog House, that Luke Magrath and Julia Brien were to be married in the following week, imbeersa; and when I reached Julia's home, that same evening, I found out 'twas a fact truth, awonomsa.

'And, sure, I suppose, 'twill be for the best, Kitty,'

ashamed of her life that she was ever seen walking with Martin.

'I suppose,' says she to herself, 'they'll say *now* that Martin Magrath is after making a fool of me and leaving me in the lurch, and he ran away with another girl, after giving all the year with myself!'

But, molaire, in this queer world everything passes out of people's minds after a week or two, when some fresh news comes this way, and 'twas so in this case, too, mossa, so it was.

And Luke Magrath hired again with the servant-girl and the servant-boy and he carried on the work of the Liscree farm, and the weeks and months went by and not another line reached him from his sister Bride, or from his cousin Martin.

And whether 'twas this trouble, or not, that was on him, a queer change came over Luke Magrath, and he got pale and thin and troubled-looking, and often, and he talking on the road, or in the bog, or even in a house to his neighbours, he'd put a start out of him, and he'd look over his shoulder, like as if he was after seeing or hearing something that frightened him and that *their* eyes and ears couldn't see and hear, the Lord save us!

And *this* wasn't the worst of it, why!

A whisper went around, mossa, that the house at Liscree was haunted and that footsteps and cries and sobs used to be heard in the rooms and passages in the dead hour of the night, God bless the mark! And the servant-boy and the servant-girl ran away home for their lives, so they did, and if Luke Magrath was to pay them down fifty pounds a week in wages the divil another night ayther of 'em would spend under the accursed roof of the old farmhouse.

So Luke Magrath was so cut-up over this that the Briens took pity on him and they asked him to sleep for a few weeks at the Bog House, and he could go over to

Liscree every day, as usual, to attend to his farm.

And, faith, he took 'em at their word, so he did and he came to sleep at the Big House every night, and the first time myself laid eyes on him, after that, I thought I never, in all my born days, saw a man so altered in his looks and manner as Luke Magrath!

The very bones in his face and in his hands seemed to be standing out from the skin, and there were black marks under his eyes, and he'd never look you straight in the face now, like he used before, and he was always starting and turning his head, like one that would be listening for something, or in dread of seeing something, God between us and all harm this night!

And, to make a long story short, why, Julia took pity on Luke, and she was kind and gentle to him always and 'twasn't long, imbeersa, till 'twas plain enough to be seen that he was mad in love with Julia—and, sure, the truth of it was, that from the very first day he laid eyes on her, Luke Magrath loved the girl, no mistake at all, at all, about that!

And, begannies, some of the neighbours were still whispering to one another that Martin Magrath was after deserting Julia and that she was pining away, after him; and, I suppose, this thought was such gall to Julia's spirit that, bejakers, she made up her mind in the end that 'twould be as good for her to marry Luke and to let them all see she wasn't dying around Martin and that she could get just as good a husband as ever Martin would be.

So, what do you think, didn't the news reach my ears, one day, on the road from Skibbereen, and I rambling back to the Bog House, that Luke Magrath and Julia Brien were to be married in the following week, imbeersa; and when I reached Julia's home, that same evening, I found out 'twas a fact truth, awonomsa.

'And, sure, I suppose, 'twill be for the best, Kitty,'

says Mrs Brien to me that night. 'Though, faith,' says she, 'I'm in dread sometimes, so I am, that Luke Magrath is in bad health ever since Martin and Bride left Liscree.'

And no wonder she'd say it, imbeersa!

Luke Magrath came into the kitchen a few minutes after that, and he looked like a man that would be fading away in a decline, God bless the hearers!—or some other sort of a sickness of the kind.

So the days went by, and 'twas the very eve of Julia's marriage, a dark, stormy night, in the month of November, it was—and now 'tis worth your while to listen to my story, and I hope it won't frighten ye to hear it!

Eamonn Brien was fast asleep on the settle in the kitchen, and Mrs Brien and her son Jack were just after going out to the cow-house to have a look at a sick cow that was in it (for the family were all up late that night) and Julia was ironing some things on the table over right the fire; and all of a sudden, why, about the hour of midnight, a rap came to the door of the scullery, just outside the kitchen door, for all the world like as if you knocked at the door with your knuckles.

'Wisha, who can that be, I wonder?' says Julia, and she opened the kitchen door and she looking into the scullery; and, 'Come in, whoever you are!' says she.

But there was no answer to Julia's words, only the crying of the wild winds around the house and the sorrowful moaning of the blast in the bare branches of the old beech-tree that was growing close to the scullery door.

And Julia stood still for a minute or two and, if she did, 'twasn't long till the rap sounded for the second time on the back door; and, 'Who's there?' says Julia out loud, and her heart and it beginning to thump against her ribs. God between us and all harm. 'Whoever you are, come in,' says Julia again. 'Sure the door ain't locked at all!'

But there was no answer this time, no more than the time before, awonomsa; so, taking up her courage in her two hands, on the mortal spot, didn't Julia dart across the scullery and didn't she ketch the door with her hands and she pulled it open wide, and, *'Who's there?'* says she again, and she opening it.

And who did she see, do you think, and he standing on the flagstone just outside of the door?

As plain as I see all of ye this minute, imbeersa, she saw Martin Magrath himself and a queer sort of a long, black cloak thrown on his shoulders, and his face as white as the face of a dead man; and before Julia got back her breath, to say one word to him, didn't the figure fade away before her two eyes and there stood the skeleton of a man, God bless the mark, and every bone and every rib of his body and they shining with a kind of greenish light in the darkness, and the eye-holes and the holes for the nose and the mouth in the skull and they giving out greenish flames, the same as if there was a fire inside of the skeleton; and at that same instant, and Julia and she nearly fainting with the dint of terror, didn't she hear a low, hollow voice, and it plainly said: *'Search the bog near the Clough Lia!'*

And 'twas the voice of Martin Magrath so it was—no mistake at all about it—and with that, the skeleton faded away into the darkness, and there was nothing to be seen only the trunk and the withered branches of the old beech-tree over right the scullery door, why! . . .

And, begannies, Julia fell down in a dead faint on the flags of the scullery, so she did, and no wonder she would, the craythur, and when she came to again she told her story to her father and to her brother Jack, and if she did, didn't they take the lighted lantern and a shovel and a pitchfork and a rope, and down with them to the Clough Lia, in the black, November night, and as true as I'm telling you my story, mossa, they never

stopped searching till they found the body of Martin
Magrath down in the bog where 'twas after lying ever
since the night that Julia fell out with Martin, just about
a year before that.

And when Eamonn and Jack carried home the body
between 'em to the Bog House wasn't Luke Magrath the
first to spot 'em and he sitting in the chimney corner of
the kitchen hearth and chatting to Julia in the turf light.
And, molaire, when Luke's two eyes fell on the dead
face of his cousin Martin—for the face was like as if
'twas only dead for a day or two, on account of some sort
of power that's in the bog-water, mossa—didn't Luke
let a terrible screech out of him, God bless the hearers,
and down on his face and hands he fell on the kitchen
floor and he made a full confession of his rascality on the
mortal spot.

And can you believe it, when I tell you that 'twas
Luke himself who was after taking Martin's life and
burying his dead body in the bog-hole below the Clough
Lia, on the very night that Martin and Julia had the
quarrel?

And 'twas all a wicked plan of Bride's and Luke's to
let on to Julia that Martin was after being false to Bride
all the rest of their cursed, lying story. 'Twas Bride
wrote the letter, with her own hand, mossa—the letter
she showed Julia, that evening by the Clough Lia and
the same night of poor Martin's cruel murder didn't
Bride hook it away from Liscree and she went back to
the County Tipperary, to live with her friends there, the
way that Luke would be saved from punishment for his
crime and would have a chance of winning Julia for his
wife, after all—and, begannies, he was very near suc-
ceeding in his scheme, why! . . .

So the end of the story was, that Luke Magrath ran
away out of the place and he was never again seen there,
good nor bad, and a story went round the country, soon

after, that Luke had gone to America; and about a year
later on, the news came that he was after meeting with
his death in a factory in Montreal.

And when this news reached the Bog House Julia was
gone away to the Good Shepherd's Convent in Cork, to
her Aunt Julia, and the poor craythur found peace and
happiness in the end and she to answer the call from
heaven that was ever and always ringing in her ears,
since she was a child.

TALES FROM AN IRISH FIRESIDE
James Murphy

'There are stranger things in heaven and earth than are dreamt of in philosophy.' In these *Tales from an Irish Fireside* James Murphy, renowned Irish novelist, tells four strange stories of curious apparitions, bewitchings, a miraculous healing and, stranger still, of presentiments of death. Drawing on all the wealth and superstition in Irish legends he keeps the reader spell-bound and leaves him wondering: what is fact and what is fantasy?

These four stories — 'At Noon by the Ravine', 'Maureen's Sorrow', 'The Midnight Train' and 'Handwriting on the Wall' are taken from Murphy's *Lays and Legends of Ireland* which was first published in 1912.

THE IRISH BEDSIDE BOOK
Edited by John M. Feehan

This is a book which will remind you of those things about Ireland that you would like to remember and read over and over again. In these pages you can let your mind wander in lazy reflection through song, story, poem, speech and anecdote with a delightful blend of inspiration, consolation and laughter.

At the end of a tiring day what better way to guide the weary eyes to sleep than with a soothing thought from the mind of some Irish writer still living, or dead a thousand years.

But *The Irish Bedside Book* is not only a bed-time reader, it is also a friend on journeys by land, sea or air — an inseparable companion for all those who love Ireland. It is a book that could truthfully be classified as one to be taken and cherished if one had to live alone on a desert island.

GLENANAAR

Canon P. A. Sheehan
Abridged by Lorna Gault

Glenanaar is one of Canon Sheehan's most poignant stories and is set in the period of the 'Whiteboy Terror'. The narrative traces to the third generation the strange fortunes of the descendants of one of the informers at the famous Doneraile conspiracy trial in Cork in 1829.

When 'The Yank' arrives in Glenanaar there is much speculation about who and what he is. Gradually his story unfolds for us in a novel peopled with unsung heroes from the ordinary men and women of the countryside Canon Sheehan loved. The people meet with ill-fortune and deliberate malevolence in the course of their lives and behind their story we see the picture of a whole people oppressed by an alien adminstration. After the final deprivation of the Famine, a new Ireland seems to be emerging, where old animosities are forgotten and a man is judged on his own life and achievements.

Throughout the book Canon Sheehan evokes for us a way of life now gone, with scenes of rural traditions and festivities. These come vividly alive and provide a background which is always authentic in its warm vitality and bleak desolation, fitting settings for the goodness and endurance of the characters who move through the novel.